The Dead Duke

Book 2 of Campbell & MacPherson

Clare Jayne

OTHER NOVELS BY CLARE JAYNE

Campbell & MacPherson Historical Mysteries

Lady Tinbough's Dilemma
The Dead Duke
A Dangerous Past
The Convenient Murder
Mr Guthrie's Double
A Virtuous Man
An Impossible Crime
The Prankster

Dumnonia Mysteries

Murder on Bealtaine Eve
A Fatal Voyage
The Vanishing Thief
Murder By Another Name

Historical Romances

Complications
An Impetuous Romance
Ladies Dancing

CONTENTS

1. AN AWKWARD MEETING

Edinburgh, October 1788

EWAN HAD not expected to be calling on Miss Campbell one day after she turned down his proposal of marriage. She and Lady Huntly were in the drawing room when he was announced and Miss Campbell looked very much as if this was not what she had anticipated either. A blush stained her cheeks as she put aside the book she had been reading and stood to curtsy to him, and there was a discomforted look in her dark eyes she had never directed at him before. He should have waited. Perhaps this whole idea was a terrible mistake.

"Please tell me there have been no new developments in the emerald necklace matter," Lady Huntly said, rearranging the folds of her dress as she sat back down on a chaise longue, and for once he was grateful for her presence and that she apparently knew nothing of his proposal. As much as she had always found fault with him, and indeed with everyone else, she eased the awkwardness of the encounter. "You were not wrong in accusing the Viscount of Inderly of murder?"

"No," he responded, accepting the seat she waved him towards with her fan. "I am reasonably confident of that business being entirely resolved."

"Then I am reasonably relieved," she said dryly.

"Our help has actually been requested over a new matter." He glanced at Miss Campbell as he spoke and saw her eyes brighten with curiosity. "A murder."

1

"No," snapped Lady Huntly, with the air of authority of someone used to being obeyed. "Certainly not. The two of you stumbled about offending everyone around you and putting yourselves in danger over the last investigation. When will you remember that you are both members of good Edinburgh society and not the kind of low persons who associate with criminals and other unsavoury characters? As for any so-called skills you may believe you possess for such work..."

Miss Campbell interrupted the tirade that looked set to continue for some time, saying sharply, "Do you not have a dress fitting to attend this morning?"

Lady Huntly turned her frown towards the elegant table clock then stood up. "I forbid any more talk of such sordid work." She aimed a stern look at first one then the other of them. "If Mr MacPherson wishes to continue calling here he should do so for the acceptable purpose of courtship and nothing else."

She swept out of the room leaving behind a silence so awkward that Ewan could not bring himself to meet Miss Campbell's eyes.

After a pause of what felt like the longest duration imaginable, Miss Campbell said, "So tell me about this murder. Who brought it to your attention?"

Her intrigued response was exactly what he had hoped for when he told Mr Fillinister they might be able to work on the matter, but her cousin's reaction worried him. "It did not occur to me yesterday but Lady Huntly may not be entirely wrong about society objecting to us looking into this. An actress has been accused of murdering a gentleman and has gone on the run. A friend of hers, another actor, has asked us to prove her innocence."

"Then perhaps we should speak to this friend and get full details of the matter, then decide whether or not to proceed," she suggested. She seemed to feel comfortable with his presence here again, the awkwardness earlier left behind, for which he was relieved. However, it belatedly occurred to him that in his eagerness to have a reason to keep spending time with her, he had never thought about the unpleasant comments she might be subjected to if they took on what would be considered a vulgar, scandalous problem.

"There must be other crimes that need solving. Perhaps this is not an ideal matter for us."

"You are not afraid of my cousin, are you, Mr MacPherson?" She spoke lightly but he could not help but recall that she had started to call him *Ewan* before his unwanted proposal.

"Terrified," he admitted readily, making her laugh, "but it is the unpleasant reaction of others towards you that I fear now."

"I attend lectures at Edinburgh University," she reminded him. "Society already thinks that I behave in a peculiar, unladylike manner. The thought of a few slights does not worry me and I presume the actress – what is her name?"

"Kenina McNeil," he supplied, "and her friend is Mr Joe Fillinister."

"I presume Miss McNeil is in serious need of our help? That there is no one else in the legal profession who might be able to prove her innocence?"

"I doubt she or Mr Fillinister could afford a good solicitor, but we should find out if anyone in the Duke of Raden's family has hired someone to properly look into it."

"If they have, it is probably they who have assumed Miss McNeil's guilt."

"Then you are right. We must find out the full details from Mr Fillinister so as to know whether or not we can help. Should I ask him to call on us here?"

"Yes, certainly, but I do have lectures I wish to attend later today. Would early tomorrow be suitable for you?"

"It would," he said.

"Then tomorrow we can learn the story of the murdered duke."

2. DETAILS OF THE MURDER

ISHBEL GREETED Mr MacPherson warmly when he entered the drawing room at eight o'clock the next morning, grateful to put a halt to a second argument with Harriette. Ishbel had known that her cousin would not be happy that she still intended to consider looking into the murder, but that had proved to be an understatement.

Fury sparked in Harriette's eyes as she made a brief curtsy then fixed Mr MacPherson with a glare. "It appears you are never far from our door these days, nor that you hesitate to damage my cousin's reputation by involving her in trying to unravel the basest of crimes."

"It was you yourself who first suggested that Mr MacPherson and I work together to solve a case," Ishbel intervened. "It is highly contrary of you to find fault now that we find we enjoy working with one another."

Harriette's glower deepened as her attention fell once more on Ishbel. "I asked you to find a missing necklace, not go running about, mixing with scoundrels and murderers!"

"We have not yet agreed to take this case," Mr MacPherson said quickly, clearly trying to calm Harriette down, which Ishbel could have told him would be a waste of time and would only result in him incurring her cousin's wrath. But perhaps that had actually been his kind-hearted intention. "And it is entirely my fault rather than Miss Campbell's that we are even considering it. It should have occurred to me that this might cause her unpleasantness from members of society."

"Yes, it should," Harriette agreed.

"I care nothing for society's opinion of me," Ishbel told her. "And I will not allow you to make my decisions for me, no matter what threats you make." Out of the corner of her eye, she saw Mr MacPherson start at this, clearly worried about just what had been said, but that was a family matter for her alone to handle.

"How you behave also has an effect on Lord Huntly and me..." Harriette began heatedly but was interrupted by the arrival of Gallach, the family's butler.

"There is a person here asking to speak to Miss Campbell and Mr MacPherson," Gallach said to Harriette, as if he disapproved of the visitor and expected the lady of the house to refuse to allow the meeting.

Not giving Harriette the chance to respond, Ishbel said, "If it is a Mr Fillinister then he is most punctual. Where is he waiting for us?"

The butler looked from Harriette to Ishbel with consternation. "He is still in the hall at present, Miss."

"Then I will show him to the library myself," Ishbel said, heading to the door, Mr MacPherson falling into step beside her.

"Isobel!"

Ishbel stopped with one hand on the door handle, the English version of her name sounding as foreign as ever to her.

"Do not forget what I said last night," Harriette told her in a low, forbidding tone. "I always follow through with my promises."

"I know." If Ishbel went against Harriette in this matter then she would suffer badly for it, but she would not allow even her cousin to control her, no matter what the consequences were. She opened the door without looking back and walked towards the strange man waiting for her, hat in hand.

"I am Miss Campbell," she told him with a welcoming smile. "Will you come into the library, Mr Fillinister?"

He gave her a graceful bow, bending low. "I'm very grateful to you for agreeing to see me, Miss Campbell." He spoke with an English accent, she noted.

He followed her into the large room where every shelf and table as well as much of the floor space was taken up by hundreds of books. Indeed, she had to move several large medical volumes – some of her own contributions to the collection – in order for them all to have a chair to sit in. Once she had sat down, the gentlemen followed suit, Mr MacPherson at her side and Mr Fillinister on the other side of a small table. Ishbel slid an unsteady pile of books to one side so she could see more of him than his head and observed him to be an attractive, slender man in his mid-twenties with brown wavy hair and blue eyes that currently held an expression of hope.

"Would you tell us everything you know of this murder, Mr Fillinister?" she said.

"Kenina – Miss McNeil – and I have worked together in the same acting company for more than a decade. As actors, no one expects a particularly high standard of moral behaviour from us – that is, if you'll forgive me for being blunt, Miss Campbell – no one cares or judges us for sometimes taking a lover. Kenina and the Duke of Raden were such companions and they were devoted to each other. You might think, as many people will, that if Kenina doesn't show high class morals then she could be capable of murder too, but she isn't. I know her better than anyone and this isn't something she could ever do. She has the kindest of hearts."

The impassioned speech made Ishbel wonder if he could be in love with Kenina. If so, then he might not be a good judge of what she might or might not do. "Neither Mr MacPherson nor myself would form any negative opinion of Miss McNeil's character because she has a romantic attachment," Ishbel reassured him, assuming from Mr MacPherson's willingness to take on the case that this was in fact true. She herself had read enough newspapers and heard sufficient conversations between male students at Edinburgh University to know more of the realities of human behaviour than most unmarried women of her age. Harriette would no doubt see this information in a different light, but Ishbel could worry about that later.

"How exactly did the duke die?" Mr MacPherson asked.

Mr Fillinister fidgeted in his chair and looked away from them. "He was found stabbed to death three days ago in the house he had bought for her."

Ishbel saw why Miss McNeil was accused of the crime. The information also made it clear that this case would be every bit as scandalous as Harriette had feared if they did accept it. "Was Miss McNeil present in the house at the time?"

"Yes. She was asleep in her room upstairs. He was in the parlour below."

"Did the servants see anything?" she asked.

"No. They have instructions to stay out of the way whenever the duke called on Kenina but she said she never let him into the house. He must have unlocked the door with his key. She only knew of his presence when a maid found his dead body early the next morning. Kenina knew she couldn't prove her innocence, so she fled Scotland, but she didn't have much money – I gave her all I had on me but it wasn't much – so she might not be able to get out of the country. If she's caught, based on him being in her house and her running, they'll hang her for definite, and I swear to you that she can't have killed him."

"Does the duke have any other family who might have already hired someone to look into his death?"

"He had an unmarried daughter, Lady Sarah Halsted, no one else. I went to her first to see if she could help Kenina but she ordered me to get out, saying she would gladly give any testimony needed to make Kenina hang."

Ishbel winced in sympathy even as she thought that it could not have been an easy encounter for the daughter either, fresh after the death of her father.

"I don't have a lot of money," Mr Fillinister went on urgently, "but I'll find a way to pay you anything you want if you'll help prove Kenina's innocence."

"We have no interest in money," Mr MacPherson said, speaking in a gentle tone to the distraught man, "only in justice. It is possible, though, that the evidence we find could actually help establish Miss McNeil's guilt."

"No," he said without hesitation. "I'm not afraid of that."

"Mr MacPherson and I will talk over what you have told us," Ishbel said, "and we will let you know if we can accept this case."

Mr Fillinister got up and bowed to them both. "I beg that you will. You have my deepest thanks for hearing me out and considering it."

Ishbel watched him leave, aware of a pleasant thrill of anticipation at the idea of solving such a case and proving his touching faith in Miss McNeil well-founded. She had been tempted to suggest to Mr MacPherson that they agree to look into the murder right away, but there were matters that needed to be resolved between them first.

3. ULTIMATUM

"HOW DID Mr Fillinister hear that we had begun to look into criminal problems?" Ishbel asked, curious, when she and Mr MacPherson were alone in the library.

Ewan looked uneasy. "There is a tavern that Chiverton, McDonald and I sometimes frequent that is popular with actors. One of my friends must have mentioned our previous case. Mr Fillinister said when he came to see me that he knew Alex, an actor friend of Chiverton's."

Ishbel listened to this with interest, curious to hear about a part of Mr MacPherson's life of which she had not previously known. She had, of course, never entered a tavern herself but knew that alcohol was consumed and card games were played in them. She had had a vague idea that they must resemble the games rooms at balls, but they clearly allowed the different classes to mingle freely in a way that would not happen at a ball. That sounded pleasant. It was a shame that ladies could not visit taverns.

"If you are willing, then I would like us to try to solve this," she said, "but there is something that needs to be resolved between us first."

"Yes, of course," he said, clasping his hands together tightly on the table and finding some difficulty in meeting her gaze.

Embarrassment swept through her as she realised his misapprehension. Of course, he was assuming she was talking about his offer of marriage. "I am talking about the wreath," she said quickly.

He blinked at her, his wide green eyes blank.

"You recall that the Viscount Inderly sent a wreath to scare you which you did not inform me about?" she said and he gave a nod of understanding, expression clearing. "I must ask that you promise never to keep such a secret from me again if we are to continue working together. I am sure you did it with good intentions, but I need no one to shield me from unpleasant information and we cannot rely on each other if we are not utterly honest."

"I understand," he said. "You have my word that I will not hide anything about a case from you again."

"Thank you. Then are we agreed to go ahead with the investigation?"

"What about Lady Huntly?" he asked, frowning. "The last thing I wish for is to cause a rift between you and your cousin."

He had reason to be concerned, but she wanted to take on this case. She liked Mr Fillinister and wished to help him. Even more importantly than that, she wanted to continue her working relationship and friendship with Mr MacPherson, something she had feared impossible after she said she could not marry him. This was a way to spend time with him and to strengthen their friendship. She might even be able to find the words to explain why she would be so unsuited to matrimony, so as to heal his unhappiness over her rejection.

"Harriette does not make my decisions for me and I do not doubt that we can resolve this." That was an exaggeration that bordered on a lie. She had grave concerns, but nothing could ever make her give up her freedom of choice.

"Then what is our first step in the investigation?" he asked with a smile that she responded to, her almost overwhelming sense of relief and happiness making her realise that she had been even more sorry than she had realised at the thought of losing him.

"Well?" Harriette asked, striding into the library as soon as Mr MacPherson had left. "Did you turn down the case?"

"No." Ishbel got to her feet. "We have agreed to solve it."

Harriette halted opposite her, eyes turning cold. "So my reputation and feelings on the matter mean nothing to you?"

"Of course they do. You are my family – I love you. However, this is something that means a lot to me. I will not give up this work."

"First, the university lectures and now this. I should have refused to indulge your whims far sooner!"

"You could not have done so," she said, angered at the very idea. She tried to reason with her cousin. "Can you not see that we are alike? You would never permit anyone to control your behaviour and decisions and neither can I."

"Is that what you believe? When you are more mature you will understand that even the most determined woman must sooner or later make compromises in order to be accepted by society. Its members do not tolerate such behaviour as you are contemplating."

"I will do nothing dishonourable. Society can accept that or it can close its doors to me. You are married to a wealthy baron; you cannot be shunned simply because we are related."

"I can as long as you are living under my roof. Censure will fall on me as well as you."

"Then you really meant what you threatened?"

"I never wished it," Harriette exclaimed. "I have put up with all manner of eccentricities in your character, but this is too much. You must refuse to be involved in so sordid a case or you can look for a new home."

Ishbel swallowed down a pang of grief. There was a part of her that wanted to give in, but that was just fear and she would not be ruled by such a feeling. Her life was in her own hands. It had to be. "Then I will leave."

4. ELICIT ENCOUNTER

"HOW ARE you feeling?" Edward Chiverton asked his mother, as he moved to sit on the chair beside her bed. She was propped up by several pillows, her complexion devoid of colour.

"I am stronger," she said, as though trying to convince herself as much as him. "I will be on my feet again very soon. Where is your sister?"

"I believe Fiona has already dressed for dinner and is downstairs talking with Father and Henry."

"Good. You must remind her to obey them without question while I am unable to chaperone her."

He heard these instructions on an almost daily basis and had the same reaction as ever. Fiona was more than capable of making her own decisions and he would trust her good sense over Henry's narrow view of the world any time. His parents would never see it, though. "Of course, Mama."

"Do not turn that innocent blue-eyed gaze on me, child. I know how you and Fiona like to plan reckless deeds, but neither of you are children anymore and it will not do. Her behaviour must be faultless if she is to make the best possible match and you must set the right example. She looks up to you more than she does Henry."

Eddie's mouth twitched at the idea of anyone admiring Henry. "If my sister requires a chaperone tonight then I will be glad to accompany her wherever she wishes to go and guard her with my life." He thought with a pang of Alex: it had been four days since Eddie had last seen him.

His mother sighed at his light tone and reached out for the glass of water on the oak table beside her bed. He leaned over to get it and pass it to her so she would not have to stretch to reach it. The smallest movements could leave her shaky and faint. She took a couple of sips and then let him put the glass down for her.

"Is there anything I can fetch or do for you?" he asked.

She patted his hand. "I have a book of religious teachings your father requires me to read and I am sure that will take my full attention."

He tried to keep his expression blank. "How pleasant."

He left her to rest and, with his valet's assistance, changed into an evening outfit, the rich blue silk jacket and breeches matching the stripe in his velvet waistcoat and the cravat folded and tied perfectly. He then followed the sound of voices downstairs, his footsteps slowing as he got closer to the drawing room. He paused, straightened and then walked inside. The curtains were closed and all the candles had been lit in the lamps, so darkness clung only to the corners of the opulent room.

"Edward, dearest," Fiona said, crossing the room to take his arm and throw him a dark look. "How long it took you to get changed."

"I was telling my sister of the dangers of copying the kind of flirtatious behaviour of certain married women," Henry said, leaning against the marble fireplace, his face schooled into an expression that was probably meant to convey wisdom, but that actually made him look constipated. "Virtuousness and innocence are what a gentleman expects from a young lady."

"And showing too much intelligence is highly unattractive," his father said, ignoring Chiverton as had become his custom since learning of his younger son's romantic preferences. He was seated in his usual chair, his clothes and white wig of an elaborate style that had been popular more than a decade ago. Eddie always thought that he looked like a king waiting for his subjects to kneel down and swear fealty to him.

Fiona's grip on Eddie's arm tightened. "I will remember your helpful advice, Papa, and yours, Henry."

And, wherever possible, ignore it, Eddie knew from long experience of doing the same. He and Fiona sometimes seemed to like cuckoos, placed in the wrong nest.

The butler announced dinner and they trailed into the dining

12

room where he discovered that he would not be required to act as chaperone this evening after all. While he did not envy his sister an entire evening in Henry's company, Eddie could barely keep the smile off his face at the thought of a night of freedom.

He took his leave of them just as his father was bestowing on Fiona a book of instruction on moral behaviour for young women. He caught his sister watching him leave with a wild hungry expression.

The butler opened the front door for him and, when it closed behind Eddie, he stood for a moment and enjoyed breathing in the cool evening air, even scented as it was with the odour of horse manure. It sometimes seemed to him that his affectionate feelings towards men were a great blessing, allowing him to break out of the carefully controlled patterns of behaviour wealthy society insisted upon and find a life that was unique to him.

A few minutes and a short carriage ride later Eddie raced up the stairs of the house where Alex rented a room, bursting inside. Alex was lounging on the bed, a thick collection of parchments in his hand, doubtless a new play. He wore only a shirt – that, when he got up and had the lamp light behind him, was turned almost translucent – along with breeches and stockings that Eddie immediately longed to divest him of. Alex crossed the room, a warm smile on his face, and Eddie caught him in his arms, swinging him round in a circle and kissing him.

Laughing, Alex said, "I missed you too." They kissed again, taking their time, and then Alex stepped away to get him a glass of wine, handsome face growing more serious. "Have you heard the disturbing news? The Duke of Raden is dead."

Eddie accepted the glass with a smile and drank half its contents before asking, "Who?"

"You remember. The duke. He came to the theatre all the time." When Eddie continued to frown in confusion Alex threw himself into a chair – on top of a couple of items of clothing – and sprawled there as he added, "He was in love with Kenina."

Eddie finished his wine and moved to lie on the crumpled bed, hoping it would give Alex ideas. "That hardly clarifies it – everyone loves Kenina. Do you mean the gentleman who bought drinks at the tavern for everyone in the play?"

"Yes. Him. He was killed."

Eddie propped himself up on one arm and stared at Alex, trying to take this in. The duke had been good-natured even when drunk and, even more unusual, had put on no airs amongst the actors, treating everyone from the troupe manager to the youngest actor and to Eddie himself like an old friend. Although he had only seen the duke a couple of times, he had liked him. "Do you mean he was murdered?"

"The town guards have been searching for Kenina here and with everyone else she knows. She's run away. They think she stabbed him."

Eddie pictured the small, vivacious actress. "That is the most ludicrous idea imaginable." Feeling that someone needed to do something to help, he added, "I wonder if my friend, MacPherson, knows about this."

5. DETAILS OF THE MURDER

IT WAS one of Mr MacPherson's footmen who, having been requested to ask around about the duke's death, had discovered that the Town Guards had been called in when the duke's body was discovered. The servant had even managed to find out the name of the soldier who had dealt with the case.

That was how Sergeant Angus McIntosh came to be sitting opposite Ishbel and Mr MacPherson in her drawing room, brightly dressed in his red uniform, black tricorne hat on his lap. He was a red-haired Highlander of fifty or so, deep lines etched into his face.

Mr MacPherson explained how they were involved in the investigation, Ishbel adding, "We just want to find out the truth of what happened to the duke."

"With respect, miss, we already know what happened," he said in a gravelly voice. "Kenina McNeil killed him."

"What makes you so certain?" Mr MacPherson asked.

"He was dead on the floor of her house. There was no one else who coulda done it."

"Surely there were servants in the house too – one of them could have killed him?" she suggested.

"What reason would any of them have? The Duke of Raden paid their wages. He was a decent, well-liked man – well, other than, you know, his improper relationship with the actress."

"Then you think Miss McNeil had a reason to kill him?"

"In a secret relationship of that nature, people have arguments. Perhaps she wanted more money from him or started running round

15

with someone else and he found out. There are plenty of things they coulda rowed about."

Then he knew of no actual reason, she realised, offended on Miss MacNeil's behalf. It did not sound as if there had been much of an investigation before the woman's guilt was pronounced.

"What exactly did you see when you were called to the house?" Mr MacPherson asked. "Where was the duke's body and what state was the room in?"

"The duke was lying on the floor of the parlour. He'd been stabbed more than once and there was a lot of blood everywhere. The maid who found him got it on her shoes and tramped it all over. She was hysterical. The actress was already gone, vanished as soon as the maid woke her up and told her what had happened."

"Surely that seems odd to you?" Ishbel said. "Why would she kill her lover and then calmly go to sleep, only to wait until the body was discovered before she left?"

"She left, miss. That's the part I took note of. Innocent people don't flee when a corpse is found. Who knows what was in her mind after she killed him? Murderers don't always act like sane people and an actress living like that was already nothing better than a wh..."

Mr MacPherson coughed and glared at the man, who looked discomforted.

"Sorry, miss. You wouldn't know about such people but a woman like that wouldn't think twice about butchering someone."

Ishbel ignored this and asked, "Had any of the servants heard or seen anything during the night?"

"No, miss. They were all asleep."

"Did the room look disturbed – upturned furniture, for instance – as if there had been a struggle?" Mr MacPherson asked.

"No, sir. It looked as if someone walked right up to him and stuck the knife in; as if he never thought he needed to defend himself."

Neither of them had any more questions so they thanked the officer for his time and he left the house.

"Do you think a lot of people will make the same assumptions as the sergeant?" Ishbel asked. "That Miss McNeil must be guilty simply because she was an actress with a lover?"

"I fear so. To be fair, while there is no direct evidence of Miss McNeil committing the crime, the information we have been given so far suggests her as the main suspect. The murder did occur in her home and the fact the Duke of Raden did not fight off his attacker suggests it was someone he trusted."

"A servant could just as easily have walked up to him and stabbed him."

"But why would they do it?"

She frowned. "We need to find out a lot more about the Duke of Raden."

"And about Miss McNeil. We have to know if she did have a motive."

"All right. We can speak to the duke's daughter about him."

"If she will even see us. Remember what Mr Fillinister said about her determination to see Miss McNeil hanged?"

"Oh, yes." The situation was an awkward one and, apart from anything else, the daughter must still be coming to terms with the nature of her father's death. "Perhaps we should speak to her later then. If we can find out when the duke's funeral is to be held, we can meet all his acquaintances and get an idea of his character."

"I will find that out," he promised.

"In the meantime, Mr Fillinister could introduce us to the group of actors he and Miss McNeil work with to learn more about her."

"Oh! I, er..." Mr MacPherson fell silent, expression acutely uncomfortable.

Ishbel was surprised by his reaction then a horrible thought occurred to her. He had already said that he knew the acting troupe and had seemed uncomfortable when speaking of the acquaintanceship. Could he also have had a lover amongst the group? Surely, when he had just proposed to her, he could not have also been conducting an affair?

6. A SECRET REVEALED

"MR MACPHERSON, is there something...? There is no actress among your acquaintances that...?" Miss Campbell tailed off, unable to complete the sentences, fear in her eyes.

For a moment Ewan could not imagine what she was asking, lost in his own thoughts of how to tell her about Chiverton, then the realisation leapt into his head. "No! I... No, I would never behave in such a way, not when I love, er..."

She blushed and gave an awkward smile. "Forgive me for misinterpreting your reaction. Such a thought would never have occurred to me, but you seemed so uneasy about visiting the actors."

"Yes. I..." He took a deep breath, knowing the explanation would be no less awkward for being dragged out. "There is something you should know, to keep my promise of not hiding anything about cases from you, but it is nothing connected with me personally, I can assure you."

"Of course not." Her cheeks were still red as she got up to ring for a servant. "Let us have some tea."

By the time she had given the butler the instructions and he had left, she was composed once more and resumed her seat, saying, "Please tell me anything I should know."

"It is a private matter affecting a friend of mine, but it is something that might well be mentioned by the actors. I do not quite know how to speak of such a subject to a lady, though."

"I do not shock easily, Mr MacPherson. Please, just tell me the facts."

"You recall my friend, Chiverton?"

"Of course."

"I have known him all my life, so we have no secrets from each other. The fact is that, well, are you aware that some men do not think of women in a romantic manner?"

She looked confused. "No, I did not know that."

"Chiverton..." He broke off as two footmen entered the room, unable to speak further in front of them. It would not have been right to keep this from her when he had promised not to keep secrets, but the rest of the conversation loomed over him as the most awkward of his life. He had no idea how to even speak of such an intimate matter, let alone explain it in a way that would not have her thinking badly of Chiverton.

The footmen bent down to place small china cups and a teapot on the coffee table between them along with plates of freshly baked shortbread then straightened and left them alone once more.

Miss Campbell poured the tea for them both, then picked up her cup and took a sip from it. Ewan did the same.

"Chiverton is a good man. I would never want you to think otherwise," he said.

"I cannot imagine doing so," she reassured him. "He behaved towards me in a kind, gentlemanly manner, even after I had shown what an inept dancer I am."

He smiled at this, remembering the first time he had seen her at a ball and how beautiful she had been, not that she was any less so now in a plain white morning dress, her copper curls around her shoulders. "Chiverton will never marry. He does not have those kinds of feelings for women."

She nodded, brow furrowed, clearly still not understanding what he was trying to say.

"Chiverton has a close male acquaintance amongst the actors."

"Oh." Silence fell and they both took another sip of their tea. She said, "When I was a child, my parents took me to church every Sunday. That is the only place I have heard the subject mentioned and, of course, not in a kind manner. It is a crime, is it not?"

Ewan went cold. He had not even considered that she might feel a duty to report this to the law and Chiverton could be hanged for the crime of sodomy. How could he have overlooked such a thing? "He intends no sin, nor to harm anyone. He simply wants to have someone to love."

"I did not think of it in those terms."

"Miss Campbell, you will not have him arrested, will you?"

"No!" she said at once, eyes widening at the idea. "Never. I might not understand this but, as you said, no one is injured from what he and his acquaintance do, so I would not dream of causing a friend of yours such harm."

He let out a shaky breath.

"Apparently I was wrong in saying I was not easily shocked," Miss Campbell said with a chagrined smile. "I thought I knew all there was to know of the world from my books and from mixing at the College with so many different classes and types of men."

"This is something even men do not usually talk about."

"Is it possible for two women to have such a relationship?"

Amused to see Miss Campbell's curiosity once more reasserting itself, he said, "I believe so."

"What is the name of Mr Chiverton's close friend?"

"Alex Aldridge."

"How long have they known each other?"

"Several years."

"And Mr Chiverton's family accept this?"

"Chiverton has an older married brother to inherit the family money and produce an heir, so his parents accept his refusal to marry. I do not know exactly what he has said to them on the subject, nor what their response was. I believe there was an unpleasant exchange with his father when Chiverton first tried to explain his feelings."

"Why is it illegal?"

"The law, as we have found, is not always fair and people are not always kind to those who are not exactly like them."

"Then I am glad Mr Chiverton has friends he can rely on."

The matter resolved, they finished their tea and shortbread in companionable silence and then took Ewan's curricle to Mr Fillinister's address. He was more than happy to take them to the playhouse where some of the troupe's actors and manager were discussing a new production. Ewan had attended performances at the theatre and been backstage to speak to the actors, but had never been here at other times. The vast, brightly coloured stadium was filled with empty seats and large abandoned stage, patches of darkness coming from the higher seats in the galleries at the sides of the room, the orchestra pit a dark hole opposite the stage. The whole arena seemed to have an air of dejection, as if longing to be filled with lights, people and applause once more.

"We are thinking of doing *A Knight's Tale* by Geoffrey Chaucer," Mr Laughton, the group's manager, said in a polished English accent, when introduced to them. He was a middle-aged man with a face that must once have been strikingly handsome and a confident manner. Ewan had seen but not spoken to him before. "But you are not here about that. Joe says you want to help Kenina, so you're very welcome to speak to anyone here. Is there anything I can tell you?"

"Did you know of the duke's relationship with Miss McNeil?" Miss Campbell asked.

He smiled at her. "Yes, of course. The Duke of Raden came to see every performance by Kenina and often went backstage afterwards to see her. He was clearly smitten."

"What was he like?" Ewan asked.

"Generous, friendly. Everyone here liked him." He fell silent, a vertical line deepening between his eyebrows, then continued in a quieter, more sombre tone. "We couldn't believe it when we heard about his death. I honestly can't imagine anyone wanting to harm him. I think a burglar must have tried to rob the house, encountered the duke and killed him in a panic. It's the only thing I can think of that'd make sense."

Unfortunately the theory did not match what the sergeant had said about the house being undisturbed and no fight occurring when the duke was killed. The actors in the arena with him said much the same thing: that they had never seen the duke in a bad mood and that he was as free with his praise as he was with his money. They ventured behind the stage area where a few more people sat about in dressing rooms, or did carpentry, or other work.

A young seamstress who said her name was Joanna had more to say as she sat stitching a dress. "Miss McNeil would never have done such a thing. It's evil of anyone to say she could be guilty. She loved the Duke of Raden. I never once heard any disagreement between them, just the opposite. In fact, he was going to marry her, I'm sure of it."

"You heard him speak of marriage?" Miss Campbell asked, a note of surprise in her voice.

"Well, I never heard him propose exactly, but he said how much he loved her and that he never wanted to be parted from her. Their courtship was the most romantic thing I ever saw – I didn't think things like that happened outside of plays, where people would do anything for each other."

They left her, Ewan lost in thought over her words and nearly walking into a familiar figure.

"MacPherson!" Alex exclaimed with a grin. "I didn't know you were visiting. Where's Eddie?"

"Oh, er, no, Chiverton is not with me," he said and gestured to Miss Campbell. "I am here with Miss Campbell to look into the death of the Duke of Raden. Miss Campbell, may I introduce Mr Aldridge to you."

She curtsied and Alex bowed to her, his playful side hidden behind a formal politeness more appropriate in front of a lady. Ever the quick-witted actor, he could adapt his behaviour in an instant to suit any situation, fitting in with people from every station in life. It occurred to Ewan that it was Chiverton's acquaintanceship with Alex that had introduced Ewan to more of the world than its wealthiest inhabitants, giving him an interest in the lives of working-class people that made him now wish to get justice for them.

Alex said, "It's truly good of you both to take this matter on. Joe's beside himself and no one here believes Kenina would ever have done such a thing. It makes no sense."

"How long have you worked in this group, Mr Aldridge?" Miss Campbell asked.

"Almost since its beginnings. I was ten when I joined, taking on any child roles in the plays. Kenina and Joe are the only ones who've been working longer for Bill Laughton than me. We're like a family, so this murder's a horrible shock to everyone."

Ewan hadn't known that Alex had grown up amongst the actors. It must have been a strange childhood, travelling around Britain and putting on performances. The group had been based in Scotland for a while now, just moving between the theatres in Edinburgh, Glasgow and Inverness, with permanent bookings in all of them. Ewan and McDonald had been with Chiverton at the theatre when he met Alex, the spark between them instant, even though Ewan had not immediately understood what it meant. Ewan would have seen the other actors on the stage, including Kenina MacNeil, at the same time but — as much as he tried — could recollect none of them, having been to hundreds of similar performances before and since.

"How would you describe Miss MacNeil?" he asked.

"She has a caring nature, enjoying looking after all of us. The duke — well, he wasn't her first such relationship but I never saw her in love like that before. Her life must have fallen apart when he was killed."

"You did not see her before she went on the run?"

"No. I only heard what had happened from Joe. The Duke of Raden was a good man: he didn't deserve such a fate."

They left the theatre and returned to Miss Campbell's house to talk further.

"If the duke had really intended to marry Miss McNeil then it would have caused a considerable scandal," Miss Campbell mused as they took their usual seats in the library, the room warmed by a blazing fire. It had been cold both outside and in the theatre, with a late autumn chill that soaked into one's bones, so the heat was welcome. "If his daughter is unmarried then I assume she has inherited all the duke's estate and wealth."

"You mean, she might have killed her father rather than see him re-marry? Surely she would have had a better reason to kill Miss MacNeil than her father?"

"You could be right, but I would like to speak to her more than ever." She tailed off as her cousin sailed into the room.

Ewan hastily got to his feet to bow to her and got the briefest of curtsies in return.

"I will not interrupt your discussion. I was simply fetching a book I wanted." She did so, expression cool as she left without another word.

The rift between Miss Campbell and Lady Huntly was clearly worse than it had been yesterday, Ewan realised, dismayed, and it was entirely his fault.

7. PUBLIC CENSURE

ISHBEL SAT around the large table surrounded by men and women dressed in silk and velvet, many of them having powdered their hair or worn a wig for the occasion. She found herself contrasting this formal dinner with her meeting with the actors earlier today, with their practical clothes and easy manners, surviving only by hard work. Edinburgh's finest lords and ladies seemed delicate and incapable in comparison.

Harriette had asked a week ago – before the investigation ever began – that Ishbel attend Lord and Lady Mulligan's dinner party with Lord Huntly and her. Ishbel had hoped that her attendance here might thaw Harriette's anger a little, but there was no sign of this so far. Ishbel had begun to make enquiries about gaining employment as a governess or school teacher and had discovered several positions she was capable of doing well. It would change her life, but she found she was not too worried about the prospect; in fact, a large part of her would be relieved beyond measure to walk away from the aristocratic world and its harsh rules. However, it would give her less time to spend with Mr MacPherson and she might have to cease attending university lectures altogether, both of which would be a painful sacrifice.

Ewan – Mr MacPherson was here tonight but seated too far away from her to be able to converse with. He looked handsome beyond words in his finery, just as comfortable in this setting as he was amongst the actors or other working-class people. Was it easier for men than for women to move freely between the different classes of society or was he unique?

His friends, Mr Chiverton and Mr McDonald, were also present tonight and Mr Chiverton had been given the seat opposite her own. She wondered if he was aware that she knew his secret; from the calm, friendly way he had greeted her earlier, with a compliment and a smile, she thought not. She was not quite sure how to speak to him now; she would never condemn him for his feelings about men, but she did not understand them.

Her attention, which had been lost in her own thoughts for the last five or ten minutes, was caught by the mention of a familiar name: "... Tinbough yesterday for the first time since his son's arrest." Mr Allen was speaking. He was a thin man of around thirty with an over-familiar way of looking at ladies who, for some unknown reason, was popular at such gatherings as this.

"I have not seen poor Lady Tinbough at any of this week's entertainments," the newly married Lady Morgan said. She could not be more than sixteen years old but spoke freely of anything that came into her head now that she was no longer under her mother's control. "Does anyone know when the trial is to be held?"

All eyes turned towards Ishbel and Mr MacPherson. "A date has not yet been set," she replied. The arrest had only been made by the two of them four days ago. They were still waiting to hear exactly what charges Lord Inderly would face.

"It is such a terrible disgrace for the family," Lady Morgan responded with relish. "I doubt we will ever see poor Lady Tinbough again."

"Lady Tinbough has done nothing wrong," Harriette said from a couple of seats further down the table, with a quelling look at the younger woman. "She is naturally distressed at the moment but will certainly attend functions in the future."

"One cannot help but feel that the matter should have been dealt with privately," Mr Allen said, throwing a challenging look at Mr MacPherson. "It would have been far kinder."

"Not for the family of the dead girl," Mr Chiverton told him, his manner decisive but amiable. "No one, not even someone from the highest of families, can be permitted to go about committing crimes. If it were otherwise, how safe would any of us feel?"

"Very true," Lady Mulligan said and, as hostess of the gathering, her words ended the public discussion.

Two seats down from Ishbel, however, a French woman who had just arrived in Edinburgh asked to have the matter explained to her. There were a number of French families settling here now, fleeing from their own country now that a revolutionary war was likely to begin at any time. Ishbel braced herself as a hushed conversation began, explaining what Lord Inderly had done and Ishbel's own involvement in the matter.

The French woman looked to be around fifty-five and wore a necklace with an enormous diamond that had received many admiring comments earlier. When she had heard everything about the case, including a number of false statements Ishbel had longed to correct, the lady said in perfect, accented English, "In France a young unmarried woman of good family would never dream of involving herself in so sordid a business. It would destroy her reputation and any chance she had of making a good marriage, but perhaps this mademoiselle does not come from a decent family."

The words were pitched to reach her ears and Ishbel's cheeks burned as she clenched her teeth together so stop herself responding to the insult. To do so would only increase the gossip and lengthen the conversation. And Harriette would never forgive her.

"Miss Campbell, what a charming dress you are wearing," Mr Chiverton said from across the table and she lifted her head to look at him. He had clearly also heard what was said against her, she realised, embarrassed but grateful. "I believe that shade of blue would suit my younger sister very well."

Ishbel had not met Mr Chiverton's sister, who was not yet out in society, but if she had the same fair hair and large blue eyes as her brother, any colour would likely suit her. Ishbel mentioned the modiste who had made the dress for her, sparking a long dull conversation about clothes and hats, for which she could not have been more happy.

It no longer mattered to her that she could not understand Mr Chiverton's feelings regarding men and women. If he could consistently be so kind and good-natured, in the face of so many people acting in the opposite manner, then she was glad to consider him a friend.

8. DISAGREEMENTS

EWAN TRIED to show an interest in the conversation of his dinner companions while becoming increasingly concerned about what was being said at the other end of the table to make Miss Campbell look so uncomfortable. He feared it was something to do with Lord Inderly's arrest and wished he could intervene.

Lady Huntly had aimed a poisonous glance at him after the slight to Lady Tinbough and he thought, once again, that he should have properly considered the consequences of him and Miss Campbell taking on the new case, particularly when it had the potential to be far more scandalous than the previous investigation.

He had thought only of himself. He had wanted to continue to see Miss Campbell and the case had been a perfect method of doing so. He had also wanted to keep resolving criminal matters. It had seemed a worthwhile use of his time and alleviated a boredom with his life that he had not previously been aware existed. However, if it damaged Miss Campbell's reputation and her relationship with her cousin, then they should cease immediately. Unfortunately he had not yet found a way to get Miss Campbell to change her mind once it was fixed on a course of action and, now that he had brought the crime to her attention, she was clearly determined to solve the duke's murder.

He glanced again, helplessly, in Miss Campbell's direction and, to his surprise, heard her discussing clothing with Chiverton and several others. She must be bored witless by such a conversation but gave no sign of it and the subject was soon taken up by the rest of the guests.

"Some people think that we French have the finest modistes in the world," the young lady seated next to him said. "What do you believe, Monsieur MacPherson? Is my dress beau?"

"It is a lovely gown," he said politely.

"And does it suit me well?" She was making eyes at him, smiling from behind her fan.

She was a pretty woman and he realised for the first time that he had no way of communicating the fact that he loved someone else and was thus unable to share a flirtation with her. He was not engaged to Miss Campbell and, unless her views on matrimony changed, might never be. Trying to put the right mixture of politeness and lack on encouragement in his tone, he said, "You look beautiful, mademoiselle."

"Ma mere said I should wear a woollen shawl but I would rather be cold than ugly. Your weather is bad, is it not?"

"It is certainly cold at this time of the year," he agreed, "and damp."

"I should not say this to a Scotland person, but I liked London better, however mon pere had acquaintances here, so we will live in Edinburgh."

"Then I hope you will develop a fondness for our home."

"Develop..?" She looked confused and he realised she had not understood the phrase.

"I hope you will like it better soon."

"Yes. When I have good friends of my own I will be happy here." She smiled at him, a hopeful look in her eyes and he felt sorry for her, alone in a new country, but he could think of no way of offering to be her friend without giving the impression that he was free to be more than that.

The meal came to an end and the assembly moved to the drawing room for a piano recital. Ewan at once sought out Miss Campbell to find out what had been said to her earlier.

"It was nothing," she reassured him. "A lady made a comment about it being unladylike for me to be involved in the solving of crimes. I am sure I will hear a great many more such opinions and will take equally little notice of them. Mr Chiverton was very kind, though, and distracted everyone from that subject."

Ewan would have expected no less from his friend and focused on her other words. "It is not too late for us to stop looking into the duke's murder or for you to take a lesser role in the investigation to protect your reputation. It would help you to mend matters with your cousin."

"I wish to solve the murder with you and would rather be scorned by every lady and gentleman in Edinburgh, including my cousin, than be afraid to live my life the way I want."

He nodded, unsurprised by her words. "Perhaps the matter can be easily resolved. I regret to say it but so far we have found no other suspect than Miss McNeil."

"We have only spoken to a handful of people," she countered. "And the duke's daughter is a possible suspect." She looked around the room with sudden interest. "I wonder if she could be here this evening. Harriette would probably refuse to tell me so but perhaps one of your friends has been introduced to her. What was her name: Lady Sarah..?"

He frowned, trying to remember. "Hartley? Hillborough?"

"Hillsted. I am almost certain it was Hillsted."

Lady Mulligan interrupted them, speaking loudly from the other side of the room to introduce the pianist. Ewan and Miss Campbell found seats from amongst the rows of chairs that had been laid out for the occasion and Ewan managed to catch Chiverton's eye and make a slight beckoning gesture. With an amused expression, Chiverton collected McDonald from his conversation with two unmarried ladies and their mothers, and the two of them took seats beside Ewan. The pianist had approached the piano by this time, though, so Ewan had to wait nearly an hour for a break in the proceedings before he could speak to them.

As the first half of the performance ended and polite applause sounded for the pianist, Ewan leaned closer to his friends and said, "Do either of you know a Lady Sarah Hillsted? Is she here?"

"The duke's daughter?" Chiverton said at once while McDonald looked blank. "I have only heard of her, but I do not think her name is Hillsted."

"I am certain it began with an '*H*'," Miss Campbell said, leaning close to him to be heard by his friends. Her arm brushed against his and he breathed in the scent of the lavender fragranced water she must have bathed in.

"Halsted."

Ewan started, eyes flying open and heart beating quickly, as he turned towards the row behind theirs.

"Her name is Lady Sarah Halsted," Lady Huntly informed them in a long-suffering tone, "and, having just lost her father, of course she is not here tonight."

"Do you know when the duke's funeral is due to take place or has it already been held?" Miss Campbell asked her cousin in an unusually timid tone.

"The service will be held the day after tomorrow. I trust I need not warn the two of you not to interrogate the poor woman at her father's graveside?"

"We will say nothing untoward," Miss Campbell promised. "Not at the funeral."

Lady Huntly gave an exasperated sigh and got up to accept the plate of refreshments and drink a young man had brought over for her. She then dismissed her young admirer and joined a select group of influential ladies, her dry comments soon added to their conversation.

"Your cousin sounded a little more reconciled to your involvement in the case, I think," Ewan said.

"Yes." Ishbel sounded relieved.

"What case is this?" McDonald asked, frowning. "Ewan, what are you up to now? Was Lord Inderly's disgrace not enough for you?"

"His disgrace was his own doing," Ewan pointed out, stung.

"In fact, this new case involves friends of mine," Chiverton said, "so MacPherson and Miss Campbell both have my gratitude for wanting to solve it. If I can assist in any way, just tell me how."

"Not you too," McDonald complained. "You heard the comments made earlier. Have you not caused sufficient...?"

"I think I will get a drink," Chiverton said hastily, getting to his feet. "May I bring you back a glass of ratafia, Miss Campbell."

"Thank you, yes."

Chiverton took McDonald away with him and Ewan said to Miss Campbell, "I apologise for McDonald."

"Why should you?" she replied. "He is not wrong about the affect on our reputations of involving ourselves in criminal matters. He is just concerned for you."

And for his own reputation through his acquaintanceship with Ewan, he thought, then dismissed the idea as uncharitable and unfair. As far as McDonald was concerned, Ewan was acting in a peculiar manner that could be damaging to his name. Ewan could not give a good explanation for his actions. He just knew that he had a greater sense of purpose now than he had had in his life before and that he enjoyed the challenge of such work. And his partner in it.

"Like you," he told Miss Campbell, "it seems that I must choose my own path in life."

"You did what?" Eddie said, his shocked reaction to MacPherson's words causing wine to spill over the edge of his glass and stain his shirt cuff. For once he did not care, the crimson mark drying while his mind was on greater concerns.

"I had to explain about the relationship between you and Alex to Miss Campbell since we are mixing with the actors and other people who know of it," MacPherson said in a whisper, even though they were some distance from anyone else in the room. "If she were to find out the truth from someone else she could do you both harm without ever intending to."

It was late and Eddie was too drunk to be able to handle such news. "She could get us hanged..." He tailed off as he imagined the rope being placed around his neck or, worse, him having to watch as Alex was taken away to be executed.

"She understands the danger and has promised that she will keep your secret. You have nothing to fear."

"What can you possibly know of fear?" he exclaimed and, with rising panic, began to walk away. He needed to see Alex. They could decide what to do together.

Ewan caught his arm, stopping him. "I swear that I will never let harm befall you or Alex over this. I would perjure myself in court rather than let that happen."

Alex took in the seriousness of his expression and the tension gradually faded from his body. It belatedly occurred to him that Miss Campbell had known his secret when they had spoken earlier and she had behaved no differently towards him than usual. "You can tell no one else."

"I will not."

"Very well." He gave a shaky laugh. "It is for the best that Alex and I will not have to flee to the continent. The heat disagrees with me."

9. THE HOUSEKEEPER'S OPINION

"IT WOULD be extremely useful to speak to the staff at Kenina McNeil's home and also the duke's," Ishbel said on the morning after the dinner party. She had been tired after the late night and had not felt like breakfast at her usual time of 7.30, so she was making up for it two hours later with Mr MacPherson while discussing the case. She buttered a slice of bread and tried to ignore her empty stomach sufficiently to take only ladylike bites from it.

"That could be difficult since the houses have presumably both been inherited by the duke's daughter. We could seek her permission to interview them but if she refuses – and, from what Mr Fillinister said, she believes Miss McNeil to be her father's killer, so that is likely – then we would lose the chance altogether. However, Miss McNeil's staff probably feels some loyalty to her and to the duke, so if we simply go to the house and ask to interview them, they may well agree."

"That is very well reasoned," Ishbel said after swallowing another piece of roll. "Shall we call there this morning?"

"Certainly. And, if we can find out which tavern the duke's staff drink at, I should think Rabbie would be willing to speak to them informally."

Rabbie, she recalled, was his valet and someone who had found out useful information for them on their last case. "By all means."

They finished their light repast and cups of chocolate and left the house. It was cold outside, with rain and a howling wind, so she was glad to see that Mr MacPherson had brought his carriage today rather than the open curricle. Gallach insisted on holding a flimsy silk umbrella over her head as Ishbel made the short walk to the carriage and a footman helped her inside. Ewan, who had braved the rain, told the coachman their destination, then opened the opposite carriage door and took a seat beside her, dripping slightly.

They reached the house that had been bought for Miss McNeil, which was of moderate proportions and was situated in a decent but unexceptional street, that probably mostly housed wealthy tradesmen rather than upper class families. A butler, dark haired and aged around thirty-five – young for such a position – opened the door to them and, in the hallway, they explained that Mr Fillinister had asked them to prove Miss McNeil's innocence.

"We all want nothing more than that," the butler said. "We will be glad to answer any questions that will help but I should apologise for the unusual state of disorder. Lady Sarah Halsted, the duke's daughter, is selling the house, so we're packing everything away."

"What will happen to Miss McNeil's possessions?" Ishbel asked out of curiosity.

"I don't know, miss. I'm reluctant to pass them on to Lady Sarah."

Ishbel winced at the thought of what the duke's daughter might do with them. "Perhaps you would allow us to take them, so we can return them to Miss McNeil when we are able to do so."

"Yes." He looked relieved. "That would be a great help. Thank you, miss. I will have them brought out for your footman to take to the carriage – there are a good number of packing chests."

"I will have them taken straight back to my home and then the carriage can return for us," Mr MacPherson said and set these actions in place.

The butler then settled them in the dining room, which showed the same signs as the rest of the house of having its contents half packed, and sent the members of staff to speak to them one at a time.

The housekeeper, Mrs Stewart, a grey-haired woman with a competent attitude, was the first to arrive and, after looking from one to the other of them in an uncertain manner, said, "I imagine you must think the arrangement between Miss McNeil and the duke was very improper, but they both behaved in an otherwise genteel way. Miss McNeil had some loud actor friends, but she never permitted any rowdy or drunken behaviour here. She also told me she took her responsibility for the staff seriously, that should any man act indecently towards any of the lassies to tell her at once and she would throw him out of the house. Not every lady would care about such things."

Ishbel thought of what had occurred in Lord Tinbough's household and silently agreed, liking the sound of Miss McNeil.

"Not that there was any need for concern," Mrs Stewart added. "The duke was always polite and respectful and none of the actors behaved badly towards the staff."

"Did the duke and Miss McNeil have a good relationship?" Ishbel asked then, blushing, realised how the question sounded and hastily amended it. "I mean, did they argue at all or seem happy?"

"They were very happy, miss. The Duke of Raden was constantly bringing Miss McNeil gifts and complimenting her, and he meant everything to her."

"Someone suggested to us that he might have been intending to ask Miss McNeil to marry him," Mr MacPherson said.

"I dinna know what was on his mind, sir, but it wouldna surprise me. Miss McNeil talked quite freely with both me and her maid, and the duke often said how much he loved her and how much better his life was since he had met her."

"Was the duke expected here on the night he died?"

"In a way, miss. He often told Miss McNeil that he would call round on a certain evening if he was able to, so sometimes he came and sometimes he dinna. We knew he might visit that night so that meant we were to let Miss McNeil open the door if anyone rang."

"Did he ring?"

"No, miss. We heard nothing. I went to bed at my usual time and the next thing I knew, the housemaid was shaking me awake, saying that the duke was dead. I dressed and hurried upstairs, thinking she must have made a mistake or that maybe the Duke of Raden had had a heart attack, and when I saw him..." She tailed off, going pale as she looked down at the dining table, as if she could see the events of that day in its polished wood.

"I know this must be difficult for you, Mrs Stewart," Mr MacPherson said, "but did you form any idea of what must have happened to the duke from the sight of his body in the parlour that morning?"

"There was blood; a lot of it," she said. "He'd obviously been stabbed but there were nae knives missing from the kitchen, so the killer dinna get it from here."

"That's very useful to know. Is there anything else?"

"None of the doors had been messed with, so we can only think that the duke let the killer in himself, if that makes sense."

"Do you have any opinion on who could have killed him?" Ishbel asked.

She pursed her lips, increasing the small lines around them. "I canna say, miss."

"That sounds as if you want to tell us something. I promise you, we will not repeat anything you tell us to another soul."

There was a long pause as if she could not decide whether or not to speak. Finally, she glanced at the open door and said in an undertone, "Aye, well... I've never seen a person less grief-stricken over the loss of a parent than Lady Sarah Halsted. That's all I'll say, miss."

It was enough to make Ishbel more eager than ever to meet the duke's daughter.

10. THE DUKE'S DAUGHTER

"WE MUST speak to the duke's daughter right away," Miss Campbell said when they had spoken to the last staff member in Miss McNeil's house. "After what the housekeeper said, Lady Sarah Halsted seems more than ever to be a likely suspect."

"Yes," Ewan agreed. "The worst that can happen is that she will refuse to see us."

They obtained her ladyship's address from the butler and had his carriage – which had returned from its side trip to leave Miss McNeil's belongings at his house – take them to the residence. The four-storey house had all the opulence that was lacking in Miss McNeil's comfortable home, but none of the warmth.

Ewan held his breath when a footman announced their presence to the lady of the house, but gave an inward smile of relief as they were shown into the drawing room. Ewan introduced himself and Miss Campbell and then said, "We are deeply sorry for your loss, my lady. We do not wish to intrude while you are grieving but we are looking into your father's death and hoped you might be able to provide us with some information, to help us find justice for him."

"The two of you are not law officers, nor members of the town guards. What possible reason could you have to be involved in such an ugly matter?" Lady Sarah Halsted remained standing as she spoke, a frown on her beautiful face. She was tall and elegant, with light brown hair and pale grey eyes that showed only coldness as she looked at them. Her plain black mourning gown added a severity to her appearance.

"We have had some success resolving crimes recently," Miss Campbell said, something she was sure they both felt true even if the rest of upper-class Edinburgh society would find fault with the description. "We were asked to look into this matter by a friend of Miss McNeil's, who hoped to find proof of her innocence, but I promise you we wish only to establish the truth. If we should find evidence of Miss McNeil's guilt, then we will pass this on to be used at her trial."

"I cannot imagine how you could fail to already perceive that woman's guilt. My father died in her ill-reputed house, with no one but the actress present."

"We have not yet established any reason for her to kill your father. He seems to have done everything in his power to make her happy."

"By that, I presume you mean that he handed over a great deal of my family's money to her," she sneered. "He was stupid enough to fall victim to her wiles and, when she found another wealthy man to dupe, she disposed of him in the ugliest manner possible."

"Do you know for a fact that she had met someone else?" Ewan asked.

"Of course not. I knew nothing of this disgusting business until a footman showed up at my door, saying my father was lying dead on the floor of that harlot's house. I need no other proof and neither will the jury when they sentence her to death."

They got nothing more from her and returned to Miss Campbell's home to discuss what they had learned. When he had helped Miss Campbell down from the carriage, Ewan sent his footman off to visit the taverns near the duke's house to find out which one the staff visited, so he could send Rabbie there later. This done, they made themselves comfortable in the library, a maid building up the fire for them and a footman bringing them hot cups of tea.

"I can see what Mrs Stewart, Miss McNeil's housekeeper, meant about Lady Sarah Halsted's lack of grief for her father," Miss Campbell said when they were alone. "Her tone, when she spoke of him, was full of only contempt and anger."

"I did not form the best opinion of her character," Ewan said, "but we must try to look at the matter from her perspective. If she genuinely believes Miss McNeil to be the killer, then she probably feels that, because of her father, she is on the point of suffering an ugly scandal that could ruin her life and damage her chance of making a good marriage."

"That is true, but I would have expected to see some sadness over his death. She had clearly not been crying at all and her attitude was almost vicious."

"It is not entirely unusual for someone to get on badly with one of their parents, but that does not mean they intend to murder them," he pointed out.

"But what if she lied to us and had indeed found out about the affair before her father's death? What if he told his daughter that he loved Miss McNeil and intended to marry her? I could imagine her capable of deciding she could not bear to lose her inheritance and killing him."

"Perhaps." He sipped his tea. "But we can do no more than guess at this point. We have no facts to support any possibility."

"We do have a few facts. We know that Miss McNeil's house was not broken into. If the duke came there with his killer, or let the killer in, then it would have been someone he knew very well and trusted."

"But do you remember what was said about the knife?" Ewan recalled. "It was not one from the house. A lady does not carry a knife about with her."

"I had forgotten that," Miss Campbell said with a frown and sipped at her tea, a musing look on her delicate features.

Ewan was thinking about what might be in Miss McNeil's belongings when Miss Campbell said, "What if the knife was from the house but not from the kitchen? Could a letter opener kill a man?"

"Probably," he decided. "If it was pushed with sufficient force, but then it would have been found with the duke's body. What did the sergeant who saw the body say about the knife? I am sure he did not mention one having been found and none of the staff mentioned it."

Miss Campbell's frown deepened. "Then it is likely that the killer not only brought a knife with them but also took it away, covered in blood, on leaving."

"The killer could have wiped it clean with a kerchief and dropped it in the room with the body. I doubt anyone would have noticed that." He considered it further and said, "I cannot imagine Miss Sarah Halsted doing such a thing but if she had hired someone to kill her father, a villain or even a servant who was devoted to her might take a knife with them to perform the deed."

"Indeed!" Miss Campbell's dimples appeared as she smiled at him.

As much as he did not want to see that smile vanish, he felt compelled to add, "This does not rule out Miss McNeil as a suspect either. She could, as you suggested, have used a letter opener, then taken it upstairs with her and removed it or cleaned and left it when she fled the house."

"But her maid said she had to shake Miss McNeil awake. Who could possibly commit murder and then go to sleep? What would be the logic in doing that when she knew she would be the first suspect and went on the run the next day to avoid being convicted of the crime?"

He could not fault this analysis. "Then I will be very interested to hear what Rabbie learns about Lady Sarah Halsted from the staff tonight."

11. THE BARON

WHILE MR MacPherson left to persuade his valet to interrogate the duke's staff, Ishbel attended three university lectures, then came back to the house to find Harriette alone in the drawing room, reading, a lit candle on the table beside her, to illuminate the dim room. Since her cousin's haughty expression was not overly fierce, Ishbel ventured to join her.

Without looking up, Harriette said, "You really must learn to wash your hands more often if you cannot write without getting ink over them."

Ishbel regarded her hands and observed the brown stains. "I had not noticed. I doubt anyone will care about that in the future. I have applied for a position as a teacher at a local ladies' school."

Harriette closed her book with a snap. "You have done what?"

"If I am to support myself then I must get a job and this is something I believe I could do well."

"You will do nothing of the kind," Harriette insisted then grimaced and confessed, "I said what I did to scare you into giving up this investigation business. Since that did not work, I suppose I will have to endure it."

Hope flared up in Ishbel. "But what about your concern – reasonable concern – over my work having a negative effect on the family reputation?"

"No one would dare insult me and Lord Huntly's friends and colleagues are academics who would never notice any scandal occurring outside their books." Her voice softened and she added, "You are a member of this family and you will always have a home here."

Ishbel abruptly found tears welling up in her eyes and wiped them away. "Thank you. That means a great deal to me."

"Hmm." Harriette picked up her book again. "My point is that, since you are remaining here, it certainly does matter if you have ink stains on your hands."

"I will go and wash them," Ishbel said, smiling.

Rabbie, Mr MacPherson's valet, was beginning to enjoy helping with his master's cases. It made an interesting change from his normal work, not that he had any complaint about that, and had brought a certain excitement to his life. The fact that Mr MacPherson and Miss Campbell had actually been able to solve their last case had been a source of much pride and astonishment among the servants and their acquaintances. Rabbie had also now met Miss Campbell and had been relieved to discover that she was a most amiable and distinguished young lady who might, in fact, be good enough to become Mr MacPherson's wife. Indeed, he could not understand why they were not already engaged.

He checked in the reflection from the tavern window that his neckcloth was tidy, took a deep breath and entered the building. It was warm and noisy inside and had a golden glow from the various lamps lit around the room. Rabbie made his way through the crowds to the bar and ordered a whiskey. Since he had no idea which people were from the duke's household, he held up his glass and made a toast, "To the Duke of Raden."

Several faces turned in his direction and a grey-haired man said, "I'll drink along with you. I was butler to the duke."

"Then I'm sorry for your loss. My master was friends with his grace and was right grieved to hear of his death."

"An ugly business," the butler said, stepping closer and a couple of footmen and a gardener joined them and also introduced themselves as members of the duke's staff. They remained standing as all the tables were full, two men starting a game of dice nearby that got a number of people betting on the outcome in excited voices.

Mr MacPherson had given Rabbie a generous sum of money to loosen tongues, so he bought drinks for them all, which caused them to treat him in a friendly manner.

"We couldna believe it when we heard he'd been murdered," Jim, a lanky footman, said. "It was a real shock. You dinna expect things like that to happen to a duke."

"Do you think the actress killed him?"

"We never met her," Mr McNamara, the butler, said. "No one in the duke's house knew what was happening."

"No, but it was obvious something of that nature was going on," Jim said. "I mean, with him going out late at night and not coming back until morning."

"Surely his family knew about it?" Rabbie said.

"His only close family is his daughter and, of course, a lady wouldn't be told of such things."

"No. That's right," he agreed and took another warming swallow of whiskey. "She must be grief-stricken at losing the duke, particularly in such a way."

"Lady Sarah is very different from her father," the butler said in a careful manner as the other men exchanged wry glances. "She was taught by her mother of the importance of propriety, so this has been a great shock. She and the duke didn't have the most affectionate of relationships, but it was just that they had nothing in common and saw little of each other."

"Nothing in common is right," said the gardener. "He was a kind man who treated everyone generously while she..."

"... She is the lady we now answer to," the butler finished, throwing a warning look at the other man.

"Let me buy another set of drinks," Rabbie said, but the butler insisted on paying this time. He accepted his new drink with a murmur of thanks and watched the other men drink theirs, hoping to get a more unguarded comment from them, since he felt he had learnt nothing so far that his master and Miss Campbell did not already know.

"Stabbing a man is not the kind of thing a woman would do," he said. "My master wondered if a thief or enemy of the duke could have killed him."

"A thief maybe," Jim said, "but no one disliked the master."

"He had a falling out with that friend of his," the other footman said.

"D'you mean the Baron Moray?" Jim shook his head. "He wouldn't stab the duke over an argument a month ago."

"The lord said his grace owed him money over something and his grace said he didn't, and that Lord Moray had been a fool. Money can make a man act daft."

It certainly could, Rabbie thought, satisfied that he might have discovered something useful after all.

12. FUNERAL

EWAN FELT like a fraud as he and Miss Campbell stood amongst the mourners at the Duke of Raden's funeral. The fact that a number of the people present were probably only here out of curiosity over such a shocking death made him feel no better.

Standing at the edge of the gathering, as the traditional words were spoken in front of the family vault, he glanced over at Lady Sarah Halsted, dressed in stark black silk with no embellishment or lace, whose only obvious emotion was annoyance. He wondered what thoughts were going through her mind and whether she really was sufficiently cold-hearted to have killed her own father. Behind her were the household staff, whose sombre expressions matched the equally bleak attire their new mistress had given them: the women in black dresses, while the men had black jackets and weepers on their arms. Ewan recognised the description of the grey-haired butler Rabbie had told him and Miss Campbell about this morning, but he had no idea which of the younger men was the talkative Jim or which was the helpful fellow who had mentioned the duke's disagreement with Lord Moray.

Amongst the crowd were some familiar faces. The unmistakeable features of judge and philosopher, Lord Monboddo, stood out. The Reverend Robertson, the principal of Edinburgh University, was there, leaning heavily on his walking stick and looking rather frail, while several colleagues stood beside him whom Ewan recognised from the times he had visited the university with Miss Campbell. Lord and Lady Huntly had also attended, as had most of the peerage of Edinburgh or, at least, those who had not yet left the city to spend the winter at their estates. Ewan wondered which of them was Lord Moray, if the man was here at all.

The service came to an end and people headed quickly for their coaches, to get out of the cold and the persistent drizzle. They reconvened at the former home of the duke, now presided over by Lady Sarah Halsted. Ewan and Miss Campbell remained in the background, not convinced her ladyship would appreciate their presence.

"Do you know which of the men is Lord Moray?" Miss Campbell asked her cousin quietly.

Lady Huntly looked intently around the room and then said, "I cannot see him."

"I will ask amongst the men," Ewan said to Miss Campbell and she promptly responded that she would find out what she could from the ladies present.

He collected a glass of potent wine, which took away some of the chill that had soaked into him outside and joined a group of men that contained a few people he vaguely knew.

"...Never saw him in a bad mood. Strange that he should have raised such a grim daughter," Mr Anders said. He was a middle-aged gentleman from a wealthy family whom Ewan knew well enough to converse with.

"That is a highly insulting comment," a young man objected.

"Och, do you have hopes in that direction, McEllis?" Anders teased him.

The young man said, "Lady Sarah Halsted would be a fine wife to any man. Her breeding is impeccable and her manners, flawless."

"And her fortune, highly desirable," commented another man Ewan did not know.

McEllis glared at him. "You are an impudent wretch, sir."

The group watched, amused, as he stalked away, heading into her ladyship's vicinity, but remaining there unnoticed.

"He can wish all he likes," Anders commented, watching his lack of progress. "Lady Sarah will be fixing her gaze a great deal higher than the likes of McEllis."

"Is there any gentleman she favours?" Ewan asked.

"Lord Glaister and Lord Stillman have both been buzzing about her, but I cannot tell if she likes either of them. The lady has an unreadable face. Why, do you want to be added to the list of suitors?"

"Hardly," Ewan said. "I mean no disrespect to the lady, but I would want a kinder, warmer disposition in my future wife."

"Sensible man," Anders agreed.

"Do you see Lord Moray? I understand he was a particular friend of the duke's."

"Not much of a friend," the younger man said. "He is noticeably absent. I gather there was some kind of falling out recently."

"Over what?"

The man shook his wigged head. "No idea."

"I know what your interest is!" Anders said to Ewan, grinning. "You are conducting another of your scandalous investigations. I have been wanting to ask the details of how exactly you discovered that Viscount Inderly was responsible for that pretty maid's death."

"Oh, that was you!" the young man said, getting out an eyeglass to look Ewan over, as every gaze was fixed with curiosity upon him.

"I cannot deny it." Ewan introduced himself and Anders gave the names of the other men present, including the young man, whose name was Lord Renford.

"Is it true that you intend to give testimony in court that may get him hanged?" Renford asked.

"I intend to tell the truth, as I understand it, over what happened to the maid. It is the jury who will decide Viscount Inderly's fate. While I feel the greatest sympathy for his family, he behaved in an unlawful and immoral manner and must pay for it."

"Then we must all watch our behaviour around you or there could be dire consequences," Renford suggested, looking half serious.

"Indeed," Ewan said in a light tone. "Should any of you have gambling debts or look lasciviously at any young lady, I will insist you be taken away and hanged!"

"But, damn it, that excludes no man alive," Anders said and they all laughed, their momentary unease around him vanishing. "So are you looking into the duke's death? I thought there was already some woman arrested for that?"

"An acquaintance of the duke does not believe that Miss McNeil is guilty and has asked us to find out if someone else could be responsible."

"So how is this Miss McNeil accused?"

Ewan glanced about, making sure Lady Sarah Halsted was not close enough to hear him. Leaning forward and speaking in an undertone, he said, "She was the duke's mistress. She is an obvious suspect, but not necessarily the guilty one."

"And who is this partner who is looking into the murder with you?"

Ewan had not wanted to mention Miss Campbell's name and did so reluctantly, not wanting to set in motion any unpleasant gossip about her. "Miss Campbell is Lady Huntly's cousin and she is working with me to solve the case. She is a highly intelligent young lady who has an interest in seeing justice done in such matters."

"I would not have thought Lord and Lady Huntly would permit Miss Campbell to look into such indelicate subjects," Renford said.

"I believe they are reconciled to her desire to help others in this way." He had been given to understand from Miss Campbell that she and Lady Huntly had now settled their disagreement and, indeed, Lady Huntly's attitude towards him today had been less censorious than recently.

The men exchanged glances over this that Ewan was not entirely happy about. Since his purpose here was now out in the open, he asked, "Can any of you think of anyone who might have a reason to want the duke dead?"

"I always found him to be an amiable man," Anders said. "Not the kind to make enemies."

The others agreed. "I heard a rumour that the disagreement with Moray was either over money or a woman," Mr Ritchley, a stout, round faced gentleman, said.

"That is hardly helpful," Renford told him. "Nearly every disagreement between men is either about money or a woman."

"Perhaps it was over the duke's mistress," someone else suggested.

"That could be a cause for murder," Anders agreed.

It could, Ewan thought, but no one seemed to know any definite facts. "What kind of man is Lord Moray?"

"He certainly has been known to appreciate a beautiful woman," Anders said, "and he has a temper. I recall one time a horse lost a race and cost him a bet, and he had the poor animal shot."

"Is he your main suspect then?" Renford asked Ewan and, once more, all eyes turned in his direction.

"Not at all. We have only just began our investigation and have no idea at present where it will take us."

"Money or a woman," Renford said in the tone of one imparting a piece of great wisdom. "Always a good place to start."

13. ATTITUDES TOWARDS LADY SARAH

MR MACPHERSON returned to the house with Ishbel and her family after the funeral and they all sat in the drawing room, drinking cups of tea or chocolate and eating sandwiches. She and Mr MacPherson had been too busy talking to acquaintances of the duke to consume the refreshments provided and warming drinks were needed by them all. Harriette also ordered the housemaid to build up the fire, which helped thaw the ice that felt as if it had got inside Ishbel's bones while they were standing outside in the graveyard.

After ten minutes, Lord Huntly took his leave of them to give a lecture at the university. Ishbel had no lectures she wanted to attend for once today, so she wanted to make progress on the case.

"What further scandals did the two of you uncover at the Duke of Raden's funeral?" Harriette asked in a tone that only held the usual amount of derision and mockery. So that was an improvement.

"I fear I ended up being the subject of questions rather than being the one asking them," Mr MacPherson said, sitting in a comfortable but upright position in an armchair. "When someone recognised me as one of the people who had caught the Viscount Inderley, the others guessed at once that I was there to look into the duke's death."

"Did you at least keep my cousin's name out of your comments?" Harriette asked as she reclined on the chaise longue.

"I fear not, but I certainly mentioned the admirable qualities that give her aptitude in such investigations."

"I am sure that will be a great comfort to Isobel when she is no longer received in good society."

"I know such an outcome would vex you," Miss Campbell said to her cousin, "but it would cause me no grief."

"In any case," Ewan said quickly, not wanting to see another

48

argument start up between the ladies, "I am sure many members of Edinburgh society would recognise that we only seek justice and would not censure either of us for it."

"You have an odd view of people," Harriette told him in a tone that suggested she would not dream of expecting tolerance or kindness from her peers.

"Were you told that Lord Moray did not attend the funeral?" Ishbel asked Mr MacPherson.

"Yes. No one knew what the basis of the disagreement between Lord Moray and the duke was. There was talk of money or a woman, but it seemed no more than conjecture. Lord Moray was said to have a bad temper and, if he had shown an interest in Miss McNeil, it could make him a suspect, but no one knew anything certain."

"It might be worth looking into."

Mr MacPherson added the names of several gentlemen who might be interested in wedding Lady Sarah Halsted, saying, "If she wanted her father dead, she might have turned to one of them to commit the deed."

Ishbel agreed. "The ladies I spoke to felt Lord Glaister stood the best chance of winning her, but more because of his wealth and good name than any feeling of affection. No one spoke ill of the duke and no one spoke kindly of Lady Sarah."

"She has just inherited a significant fortune," Harriette observed. "Of course none of the ladies like her. She can have her pick of any man in Edinburgh."

"Hardly that," Mr MacPherson disagreed. "The men I spoke to thought little of Lady Sarah's cold manners."

"They may have said that but faced with the chance to gain control of so substantial an estate, I am sure most of them would suddenly find her a good deal more appealing."

Ishbel finished her cup of bitter chocolate and placed it on its saucer, the refreshments and the dancing flames in the ornate fireplace causing a feeling of satisfaction. After their recent arguments, it was even pleasant to have Harriette's taunting comments added to the conversation between her and Mr MacPherson. "I learned that there has never been much affection between Lady Sarah and her father. She spoke to her friends of him in a critical manner, condemning his gambling, his appreciation for low entertainments and the character of his friends. Apparently he was not sufficiently discerning for Lady Sarah's taste, often mixing with tradesmen and others she did not consider to be gentlemen."

"Appalling," Harriette murmured and took another small bite from her sandwich.

"I feel more strongly than ever that she is our main suspect," Ishbel said.

"What of the actress?" Harriette asked. "Have you found out anything to firmly establish that she is not the murderess?"

"Well, no," Ishbel admitted.

"I had an idea about that," Mr MacPherson said. "I suspect you will not like it and, indeed, I am not entirely comfortable suggesting it, but we may be able to determine whether or not Miss McNeil is the guilty person by looking through her belongings. She and the duke might have exchanged letters; there could be any number of items that might show that she either had, or did not have, a motive to kill him."

Ishbel explained to Harriette how Mr MacPherson came to be in possession of Miss McNeil's personal effects and her cousin immediately said, "Then Mr MacPherson must examine them and bring anything pertinent to show you. The two of you cannot be squeamish about such things now. You either wish to do anything necessary to find the killer, or you do not."

Ishbel quashed her uneasiness of such a breach of Miss McNeil's privacy, telling herself that if her possessions proved her innocence, Miss McNeil could not object to it. "We do," she said firmly.

It was mid-afternoon before Mr MacPherson returned from his search. Ishbel had written up their findings so far, which had largely consisted of several character studies and a number of names that had question marks beside them. She had then lost herself in the pages of a medical textbook in the library, which was how Mr MacPherson found her, when Gallach announced him.

She got up and returned his bow with an automatic curtsy and looked with interest at the items he carried. "What did you learn?"

Mr MacPherson placed his small armful on a table and then hastily grabbed a tall pile of books that was nearly overturned. He took the first item from his collection and held out a bundle of letters to her. "They are only from an old friend of Miss McNeil's in England, but they provide some useful information. It would be more helpful if we had Miss McNeil's side of the correspondence, but some of her comments can be inferred from the replies. I will gladly summarise them, but I felt you would want to read them yourself. You might see something I overlooked."

She took the letters and they both sat down on upholstered wooden chairs.

"The writer seems to be another actress by the name of Mrs Philips who left the troupe when she got married. Mrs Philips often mentions the other actors, some of whom seem to have been worried about Miss McNeil's relationship with Duke Raden, fearing he would one day cast her aside and break her heart. Her love for him certainly sounds sincere, from the comments made."

"Is there any mention of a possible marriage between them?"

"No. There are joking comments about what Miss McNeil would do in such a situation, but she seems to be highlighting her unsuitability for such a position, rather than suggesting it as anything likely. She seems to have been very content in her relationship with the duke and says nothing against him."

"Then she had no motive at all to kill him," Ishbel said as she thought it over. She could not imagine how a woman could feel any security in such an arrangement, but perhaps it had suited Miss MacNeil, giving her affectionate companionship but leaving her free to live her life the way she wished.

"None that is obvious. She did, however, make some criticisms about the duke's friends. As I said, I am only assuming what Miss McNeil said based on Mrs Phillips' replies, but Lord Moray is mentioned by name. Mrs Phillips says she is glad to hear that the duke is no longer associating with Lord Moray and that Miss McNeil must feel safer because of it."

"Safer?" Ishbel asked.

He nodded. "There are no more details than that. However, there is also a mention – with no names given – of the duke's friends treating Miss McNeil with an unpleasant degree of familiarity, as if she were no better than a... well, than a fallen woman."

"That must have been horrible for her," Ishbel said. She felt as if she had quite a clear picture of Miss McNeil in her mind by this point in the case, and she liked all she knew of the woman. She was happy to learn there was no reason to think her guilty, but they still had to prove her innocence, preferably before the law caught up with her.

"If Lord Moray was indeed one of the men who behaved like that then it explains the falling out between him and the duke."

Ishbel frowned. "It is strange that the servants thought the disagreement was over money. I would have thought that they would have had opportunity to overhear the truth from the duke."

"Perhaps the issue over money – whatever it was – was the final straw, or perhaps that occurred before the duke learnt of Lord Moray's actions."

"Yes. You are probably right. Did the letters mention anything else important?"

"They give a good deal of insight into the relationships between the actors. It occurred to me as I was reading them that we might consider two sets of suspects: those who were acquainted with the duke and had a reason to want to harm him and also those who knew Miss McNeil and might, for instance, have been in love with her and killed the duke because he was a rival for her affections."

"Is such a person mentioned?"

"She apparently had quite a long romantic liaison that ended about a year ago with an actor referred to only as Tim. I can ask Chiverton who that might be."

"So if this actor's feelings had remained strong towards Miss McNeil, he might have thought he stood a better chance of winning her if the duke were out of her life."

"Exactly." He got to his feet, straightened his coat and walked to the table where he had placed Miss McNeil's belongings. "There is something else. I found this amongst the items Miss McNeil owned."

He held a small object out to her. She breathed in sharply as she took it: "A letter opener."

"It is hardly uncommon for people to possess such a thing and I can see no blood on it, but in light of our discussions about the murder weapon..."

He tailed off and she looked down at the harmless-looking silver object in her hands. Could it have been used to kill the Duke of Raden?

14. ENCOUNTER WITH LORD MORAY

ISHBEL STIFLED a sigh as she sat in the overly warm drawing room of Lady Mooreville. Since Harriette had been so generous in her attitude about her work, Ishbel had felt the need to reciprocate and had agreed to attend an informal luncheon with her. Lady Mooreville was one of the more important and well-respected members of Edinburgh society, so Harriette had felt it would be useful for Ishbel to make a good impression on her. It was only now, sitting amongst people with whom she had nothing in common, that Ishbel remembered she never knew what to say at such gatherings and was, therefore, unlikely to make any impression at all on Lady Mooreville.

A couple more guests were announced and Ishbel looked up with pleasure to see Mr Chiverton and a young blonde lady whose similarity of features suggested that she was his younger sister. He introduced her to Lady Mooreville then to the others present, smiling at Ishbel as he said to Miss Chiverton, "This is Miss Campbell, MacPherson's friend."

There was a spark of curiosity in Miss Chiverton's blue eyes as she curtsied to Ishbel, who guessed that she knew about the investigation and wondered if she also understood about her brother's relationship with one of the actors.

"I am very happy to meet you," she told the young lady. "I am never quite comfortable at big social events, but your brother's kindness has always eased my nerves. I hope you will consider me a friendly face in similar situations."

Miss Chiverton gave a pretty smile. "I would very much appreciate that. I am almost shaking with fear today and this is just a small group. I have no idea what to say to anyone."

"I have no good advice on that. I tend to say very little as I have no interest in clothes or balls."

"What does interest you?" Miss Chiverton asked.

"Books. Increasing my knowledge about medicine and the world in general."

"I like to read," Miss Chiverton said in a quiet tone, as if confessing something scandalous.

Mr Chiverton glanced round to make sure they were not overheard and then said to Ishbel, "Speaking of knowledge, how is your inquiry over the duke's death proceeding?"

"We have found a number of people who could be guilty," Ishbel told him, as his sister listened with interest. "There is actually one that we wanted your advice about. Do you know of anyone amongst Miss McNeil's colleagues whose first name is Tim?"

"Yes, Alex has mentioned him and I believe I met the fellow a couple of times socially. Now what is his surname?" He frowned into the distance and then his expression changed to a smile. "Harrison. Tim Harrison. He is one of the regular group, not one of the people whom their manager employs when they visit a new city. How is he a suspect?"

Ishbel hesitated, unsure of how much to say in front of Miss Chiverton. Trying to speak in a delicate manner, she said, "He had a close friendship with Miss McNeil, we have learnt, and could have seen the duke as a rival."

"Eddie, everything you and Mr MacPherson do these days seems to be involved in scandal," Miss Chiverton whispered to her brother. "It is wonderful!"

Ishbel smiled at the young lady's glee, certain now that she liked her, and saw her brother stifle laughter.

"It is pleasant as long as no one else finds out about it," he told her in an equally quiet tone.

Miss Chiverton made a crossing gesture over her chest. "I will tell no one."

They straightened from the conspiratorial huddle as Lady Mooreville approached to collect Miss Chiverton and introduce her to the new arrivals.

Left alone with Mr Chiverton, Ishbel found herself uncertain what to say.

"MacPherson said that he had told you about Alex and me," Mr Chiverton said in so much of an undertone she could barely hear the words. "I am grateful to you for promising not to tell others about it."

"Of course," she said at once. "I would never wish any harm to befall you or your friend." After a moment she added, "I have to admit that it is one of the few subjects I have never encountered in my book collection."

He smiled in a self-conscious manner. "I imagine not."

She found she wanted to understand him. "Is it like being in love?"

"It is exactly that," he told her. "It is the desire to find someone who loves you, understands you and will always support you that I imagine most people feel."

She digested this, thinking that perhaps the two of them were not so different: him in his wish to love whom he chose, and her in her wish to live her life as she chose. At least she was free to be honest, even if it meant facing the scorn and anger of others. It must be painful to always have to keep part of one's life a secret. "I wish you well," she told him sincerely and received a bright smile in return.

The guests had now all arrived, so they sat down together in the stiff-backed drawing room chairs and no further secret conversations were possible. Ishbel, sipping a cup of tea, was steeling herself for a dull afternoon when she heard one of the gentlemen across from her addressed by name.

With a surge of excitement, she said in what she hoped was a calm tone, "Are you Lord Moray, sir?"

"I am indeed."

For some reason she had not expected him to be so young: perhaps in his mid-twenties like Mr MacPherson. Since there was no one about who could effect a proper introduction, Ishbel ignored convention and gave him her name. She then said, "I believe I should offer you my condolences, sir. I understand you were a good friend of the Duke of Raden."

She noticed as Mr Chiverton and his sister looked sharply in her direction, clearly realising this was someone involved in her investigation, while Harriette gave her a warning glare.

"His death was a great loss," Lord Moray said, looking uncomfortable.

"And such a terrible tragedy."

"True."

Ishbel was burning with questions to put to him, but none of them were suitable for asking at a tea party and he clearly had no wish to discuss the matter. Frustrated, she resolved to simply learn more about him. At the very least, she knew what he looked like now and had exchanged an introduction, so she could speak to him further in the future.

He began a conversation with a gentleman opposite him and she studied him.

Her comments had clearly discomposed him, which was interesting.

15. THE DUKE'S INTENTIONS

EDDIE CHIVERTON CHECKED his appearance in the full-length gold-framed mirror in his bed chamber and frowned. "Would the yellow striped coat and breeches be more suitable, do you think?"

Anders, his valet, an older man of around thirty years, whose opinion on fashion Eddie knew he could trust, said in his English accent, "Either colour and style is entirely à la mode but the blue is more distinguished on you, I feel, sir."

"Good." Eddie turned and smiled. "I would not want my friends to think me shabbily turned out."

"Of course not, sir." Anders did not shudder at the idea, but the implication was there.

"I will visit Mama before I leave. Is my father around, do you know?" Eddie would rather remain elsewhere by preference or, at least, be forewarned if he was about to be ordered on some family errand.

"Mr Chiverton and Mr Henry are in the study, sir. I believe new estate accounts arrived that they are discussing and past experience suggests they will be occupied in this manner for some time."

Trust Anders to know every detail. Eddie ignored the unpleasant feeling of being kept out of his family's business affairs; he should be used to it by now. He had a generous allowance and assumed that his father or brother would inform him should the family ever lose its fortune. Beyond that, the subject was kept a mystery from him, Mama and Fiona and he sometimes felt he shared the status of one of the family horses: treated well but owned and put to use when needed. His opinion upon any business matter was as likely to be sought as would that of a horse.

He dismissed the subject and gave a nod of thanks to his valet before leaving the room. He walked down the corridor past a collection of family portraits, which showed his ancestors to have been a well-favoured group. Some, he had always been amused to see, looked smugly aware of the fact.

His mother was still confined to her room but was, at last, regaining her strength. Today she wore a red woollen morning dress and sat by the fire embroidering, the flames giving her complexion a colour that almost made it seem as if the months of illness and fear for her life had never occurred.

The sight made Eddie smile as he approached her and bent down to kiss her cheek. "How well you look, Mama."

"It is pleasant to have a fresh view of the room," she said, touching his hair as he knelt beside her chair. "I am greatly looking forward to the time when I can take a walk around the gardens."

"It will not be too many days before you can do so, I am sure, and I hope you will give me the pleasure of escorting you on your perambulation."

"That would be lovely." Her eyes hovered with uncertainty upon his clothes. "It is a cold day. Are you dressed sufficiently warmly for a day outside with your friends?"

"I will wear my greatcoat and we will be walking for much of the time, so I will be well." McDonald wanted to buy a new stallion and had asked for his friend's advice on the two possibilities.

"I can never think of Mr MacPherson and Mr McDonald as men: in my mind they are still young boys full of energy and excitement. Do you remember how little Ewan used to love seeing the ducks on our pond?"

He laughed as the image contrasted with MacPherson's current hobby of pursuing both criminals and Miss Campbell. "I recall it vividly."

A movement in the doorway made him turn his head, to find a footman hovering there. "Please forgive the interruption, Mrs Chiverton, but Mr McDonald's carriage is here to collect Mr Edward."

"Then you must not keep him waiting," his mother said to Eddie.

"I will see you when I return," he promised before leaving her and hurtling down the stairs in a manner that would have gained him a reprimand if either his father or brother saw him. Happily, they did not.

Both men were already in McDonald's carriage when Eddie got

up beside them. He had got the impression that MacPherson had been avoiding McDonald lately over the latter's cool attitude towards Miss Campbell and disapproval over MacPherson's interest in solving mysteries. He hoped the matter could be resolved today, the friendship between them all too close for such quarrels. No one knew them better than they knew each other.

McDonald handed him something that turned out to be a hot brick wrapped in wool. "My mother suggested we bring them," he said, echoing the concern of Eddie's mama, "and I think she was right. I had not realised quite how icy it was."

The weather was sunny but freezing and, while the carriage protected them from the wind, it did nothing to alleviate the chill, so Eddie placed the brick on his knees, hands resting on it, and appreciated the warmth it provided. Mothers clearly understood such matters and he thought, not for the first time, that the death of MacPherson's mother must have been a hard loss. Men often seemed to look for motherly qualities in wives in such circumstances, but Eddie could not imagine Miss Campbell thinking to arrange for MacPherson to have a hot brick to take on a cold carriage ride. She might remind him to carry a sword or pistol in case of unexpected danger, but that was hardly the same thing. As much as Eddie liked and respected her, he was still not certain she would be a good wife for his friend. On the other hand, would his friends think Alex the ideal companion for him? It was hardly likely, but MacPherson at least had kept any such opinion to himself and allowed Eddie to make his own choice. It was only right for Eddie to do the same.

The carriage pulled away from his house, moving at a sedate pace along the city streets that were hampered by slow-moving sedan chairs, hand-held carts and people crossing to the opposite pavement in a leisurely manner.

"How is your mother?" MacPherson asked him.

"Still resting but the physician says she will make a full recovery soon. She hates missing my sister's first public engagements, though."

"Yes, of course," McDonald said. "Miss Chiverton is now sixteen. Have you fixed a date for her formal coming out ball?"

"We will do so as soon as my mother is entirely well. In the meantime, Fiona is enjoying some informal gatherings." He glanced over at MacPherson. "Miss Campbell made an excellent impression on my sister. You had not said she would be at Lady Mooreville's luncheon."

"I did not know," MacPherson replied.

"Or you would have attended?" Eddie suggested.

"Perhaps."

Speaking mostly in jest, he said, "Fiona requested that I pass on her earnest desire to assist in any way in your investigation."

"Good gad!" McDonald exclaimed in an irritated tone.

Eddie ignored him, adding, "She thinks the work you and Miss Campbell are doing is the most exciting thing she has ever heard about."

"Have neither of you the slightest good sense?" McDonald snapped and then said to him, "You should not speak of such things to your sister, let alone put the idea into her head that it is acceptable for a lady to be in any way involved in such sordid matters."

"Miss Campbell is a lady," MacPherson said, a note of warning in his voice.

"I was not suggesting otherwise," McDonald responded in a more moderate tone. "She is a grown woman and her decision to scrutinise criminal matters – whatever I might think about it – is her own. Miss Chiverton is barely more than a child and Chiverton has a responsibility for guiding her behaviour and thoughts."

His father and brother clearly saw the matter in that way but Eddie, perhaps because his opinions and feelings mattered so little to them, was protective of his sister's need to have some say in her own life. "Fiona is a sensible girl and, of course, I would not actually wish for her to see dead bodies or converse with criminals, but I would never dream of imposing my will upon her. She knows my secret and understands that there is more to the world than entertainments and dresses. I would be glad to see her form a friendship with Miss Campbell, whose intelligence could expand my sister's own knowledge and help her with the decisions about her future she will likely make soon."

MacPherson looked touched by these words and gave a nod of gratitude to him.

"I would think better of Miss Campbell if she had not got MacPherson involved in work that could ruin his good name and cause the worst of scandals," McDonald said.

"In fact, it was Lady Huntly who first got us involved in that work, something I am sure she now regrets, but she seems to understand – as you do not – that Miss Campbell engages in such inquiries from the purest motives. Miss Campbell wants to help people whom the law will not assist to find justice, as do I."

"And I have to say, old fellow," Eddie said to McDonald, "that it is easier to find fault with others than to live a blameless life oneself. Has the fear of causing scandal ever stopped you from visiting ladies of certain establishments? Did it stop you, in your youth, gaining money to pay off gambling debts from a most disreputable source?"

"That is not..." McDonald began and then he grimaced. "I suppose that is not an entirely unfair comparison. I do not understand MacPherson's desire to involve himself in such work, but that is unimportant. I have no desire to quarrel with either of you, but you, Chiverton, can be discreet, just as I can. Publicly flouting the rules of society and sending its members to gaol could ruin MacPherson's standing in society. I am just worried you might one day bitterly regret what you are doing now," he added to MacPherson.

"I appreciate your concern," their friend responded. "I value your opinions and would never dismiss them lightly. However, this is something that I feel is larger than me. I can help find justice for people. Miss Campbell and I solved the death of a young working-class woman, a death that no one else was willing or able to look into it. We did something that helped her family and that I feel somehow gave her spirit peace. I will never regret involving myself in such work, whatever the consequences to my name."

"Very well," McDonald said, with a shrug of surrender.

Eddie looked from one to the other of them and, seeing signs of both returning to their former good humour, gave a quiet sigh of relief. For the first time, it occurred to him to ask, "Where precisely is it that we are going?"

Ishbel had attended lectures all day, forgetting about the investigation until she was preparing for bed that evening. She was due to see Ewan early the next morning so, thinking she should have something to discuss with him about the case, she picked up the bundle of letters from Miss McNeil's friend. She settled under the blankets of her four-poster bed and unfolded all the letters, to check the dates. More than half of them had been written before Miss McNeil arrived in Edinburgh or met the Duke of Raden, so she put these to one side and, out of the rest, selected the earliest.

The writing had a childish quality, with some letters spelt backwards and numerous mistakes made, and the words grew smaller and smaller towards the end of the page, since the writer had clearly not wanted the expense of paying for the delivery of more than one sheet of paper. The letter read:

My Dear Frend,

Paul and the Girls send their afectionite regards and want to hear all about Edinbora. I want to hear all about your Duke! Has he given you any moor gifts? I am not serprized that Tim is upset over it. He wanted to wed you so of caws he dislikes seeing other men cort you. Tis a dificalt thing for him but he will recuver and so will Joe and Alex hoo just want to protect you.

What are the rich gentilmen and ladys wearing...

Ishbel skimmed the rest of the letter but there was nothing more that was pertinent to the case. She picked up the next, ignored the greeting and family comments, and read:

Tell me evreyfing abowt the howse the Duke has bawt you. Is it very grand? I no he has sed he luves you but be carefull not to expect to much. He is a Duke and mite cort a rich lady for wedding...

They had not considered that, Ishbel realised, dwelling on the idea, but then she had assumed that if the duke loved Miss McNeil, he would not show an interest in another woman. However, upper class marriages seldom had anything to do with love, so what if he had intended to re-marry but not, as they had been led to believe, to Miss McNeil?

She perused the rest of the letters, reading several more comments that she wanted to talk over with Ewan the next day. She wanted to add more suspects and ideas to her notes on the case, but the pages were downstairs in the library and, while her bed was warm, the air outside it was frigid. She was still telling herself to get up when she fell asleep.

16. HUMILIATION

ISHBEL HATED Harriette. She had wanted to re-read Mrs Phillips' letters this evening and make more notes on the case based on her own new ideas and those of Mr MacPherson. Instead she had somehow been talked into attending a ball. She had certainly not agreed to it last week, whatever Harriette insisted. She sat morosely as Lucy teased her curled hair into a sufficiently grand shape and thought of all the things she would rather spend the next few hours doing, which was just about anything. There was still so much to be discovered for the case...

"Is something wrong, miss?" Lucy asked.

"On the contrary," Ishbel said, smiling. "I have just realised that the ball is an excellent opportunity for Ewa – Mr MacPherson and me to find out more about the duke. There are bound to be acquaintances of his there, perhaps even Lord Moray."

"Couldn't you just enjoy the dancing for once?" Lucy suggested.

Ishbel looked blankly at her. "Enjoy it?"

Lucy sighed and went back to her work.

"We must arrange to speak to the actors again as well," Ishbel said, thinking aloud. "I suppose Mr MacPherson could talk to them at the tavern they frequent, but I would be sorry not to hear the conversation."

"You will be careful, won't you, miss?" Lucy said. "It was one thing to look into a jewel theft that helped the upper classes but mixing with actors and killers could ruin your reputation."

"But I want to help an innocent, working class woman," Ishbel said, surprised at the warning from such an unexpected person. "Surely you understand that I wish to do only good?"

"I do see that, miss, and it makes me think better of you than ever, but good intentions mean nothing to most people. They will see only that you're behaving in an unladylike manner, which no one of your class is allowed to do, and they'll do their best to destroy you for it."

As she, Harriette and Lord Huntly left in their carriage for the ball, Ishbel found herself thinking about Lucy's warning, for some reason taking it more seriously than she had taken similar comments from Harriette and Mr MacPherson. But she was willing to take the consequences of her actions, she told herself; she had already been prepared to find a job and give up her place in high society. What more could they take from her?

Her mood remained uneasy as she entered the ballroom and surveyed the crowd of exquisitely dressed ladies and gentlemen, but then she saw Mr MacPherson and the concern faded away. He approached her, his two friends by his side.

"That is a lovely gown, Miss Campbell," Mr McDonald said in a friendly manner that was the opposite of his previous attitude.

Confused but pleased at the thought that another of Mr MacPherson's friends might be improving his opinion of her, she smiled at him and said, "Thank you, sir." She then asked Mr Chiverton, "How is Miss Chiverton enjoying society so far?"

"I believe she is starting to feel a little more confident. She would very much like to pay you a morning call soon."

Ishbel smiled. She had never had a female friend amongst the upper classes before, but she had liked Miss Chiverton exceedingly. "I would enjoy that very much. Perhaps I might write to her and suggest a day and time as I am, otherwise, frequently not at home and I should hate for her to call when I am not there."

"I am sure she would welcome that."

"If you plan to dance at all this evening," Mr MacPherson said to her, "it would give me great pleasure to claim one."

Ishbel held back her immediate denial and decided to take Lucy's advice and try to enjoy tonight. It had begun well, after all. "Yes. I believe I will dance a little."

Mr Chiverton and Mr McDonald promptly added their own requests, which she accepted with a touch of nervousness, remembering belatedly that she was in fact quite a bad dancer. When the music for the minuet began, though, she found herself enjoying the feeling of Ewan – Mr MacPherson's hand on her gloved one and the sensations provoked when they stood close together and looked into each other's eyes. Astonishingly, she found herself sorry when the music ended.

In this mood, she threw herself into the next two dances with Mr Chiverton and Mr McDonald, who distracted her from worrying about getting her steps and hops right with good-natured conversations. So she found that she had engaged in three entire dances and two hours had gone by without her feeling self-conscious or once wishing she was elsewhere.

Even Harriette approached her to comment, "Your dance skills are finally improving."

From her cousin this was a considerable compliment and further improved Ishbel's mood. She was then joined once more by Mr MacPherson and Mr Chiverton and they were discussing the letters from Miss McNeil's friend, when a young lady and her mother approached.

"Monsieur MacPherson," the young woman said, smiling up at him, "I am so happy to renew our acq-acquaintance." She stumbled slightly over the last word, this sounding like a phrase she had memorised. "I had hoped you would call on me by now."

Ishbel froze at these words, as the woman's mother berated her for being too familiar. Mr MacPherson introduced them to Ishbel and Mr Chiverton as the Comtesse Moreau and her daughter, whom he had met at Lord and Lady Mulligan's dinner party recently. Ishbel recalled the event, where she had been insulted and Mr Chiverton had helped her, and realised Mr MacPherson must have been seated beside Mademoiselle Moreau over dinner. The young woman had clearly enjoyed the meeting, making no effort to hide her admiration for him.

"I hope you are both settling in your new home and that the weather does not offend you quite so much," Mr MacPherson said to Mademoiselle Moreau with a warmth in his manner that bothered Ishbel.

The French lady laughed. "I am liking it better every day, even more so if I might be enjoying the chance to dance tonight."

"If you are willing, I would be happy to share the next dance with you," Mr MacPherson responded.

The two of them soon left to head to the dance area while the Comtesse excused herself to speak to another new acquaintance.

"He is simply being polite. He is not the kind of man who could hurt anyone's feelings with a rebuff," Mr Chiverton said to her as they watched the dance begin, the young mademoiselle moving with a grace and expertise that Ishbel could never achieve.

"He is free to do as he wishes. He has no commitment elsewhere." She had turned down his offer of marriage, she reminded herself. She had no right to object if he now looked at other women and she had always known that society viewed him as an eligible catch. She had not known, however, that it would make her heart clench and hurt so much.

She looked away and saw Lord Moray watching her. Although she had no liking for him, she at once smiled in his direction, feeling that at least she could accomplish something worthwhile by trying to find out more about his falling out with the Duke of Raden.

He approached her to say, "Miss Campbell, how charming you look."

"It is good of you to say so, my lord."

They spoke of trivialities for a few minutes, Mr Chiverton remaining at her side in a protective manner, which she was glad of given the strong smell of whiskey surrounding the lord. Mr Chiverton, of course, knew of Lord Moray and why she was conversing with him.

"It must be difficult for the Duke of Raden's daughter to be unable to enjoy balls and other such entertainments during her period of mourning for him."

An emotion entered his eyes that was gone before she could recognise it. "I never had the pleasure of dancing with Lady Sarah. We did not often attend the same functions."

She interpreted this as meaning that the duke's daughter did not like him. "May I ask, sir, if you believe that Miss McNeil killed the duke? It does not seem possible for a lady to behave in such a way."

"Kenina? As I am sure you are aware, she was hardly a lady and I do not doubt that she killed him. She was interested in his money, nothing more. When his interest in her waned and she realised she would lose everything, she doubtless killed him in a moment of rage. Such things happen more often than a young woman like yourself would know."

"It must be difficult for you, knowing that you can never resolve your differences with him."

"Raden was a charming, likeable fellow on the surface, but he took no responsibility for his actions. If a problem arose, even one he had brought about himself, he walked away from it. He caused his own death." Lord Moray seemed to finally realise that, in his semi-inebriated state, he was speaking too freely and abruptly excused himself and walked away.

"Did you hear the same thing as I did?" Ishbel asked Mr Chiverton.

"His words did almost sound like a confession or, at least, an admission that he knew exactly what reason had been for the Duke of Raden's murder."

Ishbel turned, eager to find Mr MacPherson and share this with him, only to see that he was still engaged in his dance with Mademoiselle Moreau, both of them looking happy and animated. Her excitement melted away and she felt sick. Mr MacPherson owed nothing to her because of the decision she had made, a decision that felt utterly wrong at this moment.

She pulled her gaze away from the sight and saw that the circle of people Harriette was currently conversing with included a woman Ishbel had spoken to after the duke's funeral. Mr Chiverton accompanied her as she joined her cousin, listening for a while to the comments being made, before saying to the lady, "This is a more pleasant way to spend time than when we last met, is it not?"

"Do you think to trick me again into helping with your vulgar interest in this crime?" the woman – Ishbel could not even recall her name – said in a loud tone, making everyone present look in their direction. "I have heard all about what you did to poor Viscount Inderly and his family. You are a disgrace! Propriety clearly means nothing to the child of so brazen an adulteress as your mother."

Ishbel gasped, feeling as if she had been slapped. She had believed that her mother's behaviour had affected only the family, that it had been concealed from the rest of the world, but she had been wrong. There was something different in the sounds around her and she realised with horror that the dance had come to an end.

She looked round, the nightmare moment seeming to last forever, the subject of every shocked stare, and her worst fears were confirmed: Mr MacPherson had heard what had been said about her family.

17. HAUNTED BY THE PAST

"HOW ARE you this morning?" Ewan asked, although the answer to the question was obvious.

Miss Campbell's complexion was colourless and there were dark smudges beneath eyes that were normally full of life but now held a pain that he ached to remove. "I am very well," she said, her gaze reaching no further up than his cravat. They sat down in the library, Miss Campbell choosing a seat that was further away from his own than usual, with a table between them. "In fact, we may be close to solving the duke's murder. Did Mr Chiverton tell you what Lord Moray said?"

"Er, no." That was the last thing he cared about right now. "Lady Selney had no right to speak to you in such a way last night..." Lady Huntly's subsequent rebuke had brought the woman to tears and reminded everyone present that they could not insult Miss Campbell without bringing down her fury, a lesson he felt sure most had taken to heart. It had caused in him an unexpected liking for the caustic Lady Huntly.

"... I think Lord Moray had drunk too much or he would not have said so much," she interrupted him, the reddening of her cheeks making her overall pallor even more evident.

She clearly could not bear to speak of what had happened so – despite his desire to reassure her that the words had not mattered to him except in his desire to shield her from such unpleasantness and that a number of important ladies had reacted with displeasure to Lady Selney's outburst – he could not bear seeing her further distressed, and so he went along with her change of subject. "What did Lord Moray say?"

When she repeated the exchange, he said, "It might indeed have been an admission that he murdered the duke. I wish we knew more of the quarrel between them."

"He must have other friends. Perhaps you could find out if they know anything about it."

"I will visit my club and learn what I can."

"Lord Moray's comment about the duke not taking responsibility for the troubles he caused also seems important."

"It might take us back to Miss McNeil as a suspect if the duke really did intend to leave her, although that seems contrary to everything we have learned so far about their relationship."

"Yes," she agreed, hands tightly clasping one of the books on the table in front of her, knuckles white. "Perhaps that was only what he wished to believe, if he really did have an interest in Miss McNeil himself."

"Possibly and we still have a number of other suspects to consider."

"Lady Sarah Halsted and anyone she might have persuaded to act for her. The actor, whose full name Mr Chiverton told me is Tim Harrison, who might have still been in love with Miss McNeil. We should speak again to the actors or perhaps you could do so at the tavern you said they visited."

It was unusual for Miss Campbell to want him to speak to people alone. Did she want to distance herself from the investigation? He could hardly blame her for such a wish, given the reaction last night. Indeed, he was the one at fault for ever asking her to help him solve a case that was steeped in scandal. He had been a thoughtless idiot. Worse than that, his actions had brought about her current pain and there was nothing he could do to ease it.

He reluctantly took his leave of her and drove his curricle to the club he sometimes visited, determining that, if she would not allow him to offer her his support, he would show through his continued presence in her life that the words at the ball had changed nothing between them.

How was it she had not known of her own family's public scandal?

Ishbel was still in the library several hours after her meeting with Mr MacPherson, doing nothing but dwelling on matters she usually avoided remembering.

She could never recall a time when her parents had been happy together. Her father had spent nearly all his time at the university and her mother... Ishbel could not recall when she had first learnt of her mother's affairs. Most of her memories of that time were of her parents screaming at each other and one occasion had been worse than any of the others. She had crept out of her room and sat on the cold wood of the staircase, listening to the raised voices that came from the drawing room below.

"How dare you embarrass me this way?" Papa had exclaimed. "At least try to act like a lady, even if you are not one."

"What do you expect me to do?" Mama shouted back. "You are no husband to me. You shut me in this vast cage and want me to stay here, alone and unloved. I have nothing! You have stolen my life away..."

Nothing? Ishbel blinked back tears. She had known her mother had little interest in her, but it was far worse to hear that she had no worth at all in Mama's life.

"You are being over-dramatic as always," Papa exclaimed. "I provide lavishly for your needs. You see your friends..."

"... Women you deem fit company for me! You must control everything!"

Then came the sounds of chairs and tables scraping on the wooden floor and being knocked over. A woman's shriek and the louder thud of a body landing on the floor. Sounds of sobbing. Ishbel had run to her room and pushed herself into the tiny space between her bed and clothes trunk, hands over her ears, tears running down her face.

"There you are!"

Ishbel flinched as the voice pulled her out of the past. Her cousin was standing in the doorway of the library, a frown on her face. Nothing ever seemed to intimidate or frighten her and Ishbel wished she had her cousin's strength.

"Do you really intend to hide away in the house for the foreseeable future?" Harriette asked her. "Had I known you were so easily cowed, I would certainly have found a way to prevent you taking on this investigation."

"Are you not angry with me?" she asked, ignoring the deliberate provocation. "You should be furious. You warned me this would happen, that I would embarrass our entire family by getting involved in this case, and you were right."

"I also said that if you were determined to go ahead, I would stand by you. That woman last night made far more of a fool of herself than she did of our family. Neither one of us can be held accountable for your mother's indiscretions and, indeed, they were no worse than the behaviour of countless others. I doubt there was a single person at the ball who did not have some relation – present or past – who had had a scandalous affair or two. Damage can only be done to us if you act as if you have a reason to be ashamed."

"I thought only Papa and I knew of my mother's affairs."

"Put it behind you," Harriette insisted. "The blame is not yours to shoulder. Go out and question people or whatever it is that you do and carry on with your life."

She nodded, realising her cousin was right: it would do no good to continue to sit here and feel embarrassed and miserable. The worst had been said and now she must deal with it. "I will."

As she walked upstairs to collect her hat, gloves and coat, she could not help but think that her life was not what it had been. Mr MacPherson must be so happy now that they were not promised in marriage and his friends, who had finally begun to like her, must be wishing none of them had ever met her. She had, however, chosen her own path and, whatever comments were made, she would see this search for a murderer through to its end.

18. CAUGHT

"HOW IS Miss Campbell?" Chiverton asked.

Ewan had sent a note earlier today asking his friends to join him at the tavern where Alex and the other actors came. It was early but the place was full of noise, rowdy behaviour and the smell of alcohol. Every type of person was here, from lords to tradesmen to the lowest paid worker; there were even a few women, some getting a drink with friends after finishing their jobs for the day, and others in even heavier make-up than the actors wore on stage, looking to find a paying man and begin their work for the night. There were card games, dice being rolled, bets being placed, people shouting across the room to each other and a dog barking excitedly in a far corner.

"She refused to speak of what happened at the ball," Ewan answered his friend, speaking more loudly than usual to be heard over the background din. He had called on Miss Campbell this afternoon, but she had been out. The memory of her distressed face this morning would not leave his mind. "You were both right. We should never have begun such investigations. It is my fault that she was subjected to such a scene."

"I believe Miss Campbell is a woman who makes her own decisions," Chiverton said. "If you had refused to have anything to do with such work, she doubtless would have gone ahead on her own."

Ewan smiled, acknowledging the truth of this. "That is very possible."

Chiverton nudged him and gestured to someone across the room from them. "You see that fellow in the pale blue jacket?"

Ewan glanced through the crowd to the group of actors who had just come in, eyes landing on a slender man of around thirty years, with unremarkable features and a good-natured expression. The cut and quality of his clothes marked him as working-class. "Yes. Who is he?"

"That is Tim Harrison, the man Miss Campbell was asking me questions about. I gather he has some romantic feelings for Miss McNeil."

"They had an affair that ended about a year before her involvement with the duke. I want to discover if his feelings for her faded or not, in case he could be guilty of the murder."

"Then this is a good time to find out," Chiverton said, waving to catch Alex's eye. His lover grinned, handsome face lighting up, and approached, a few friends with him although not, unfortunately, Tim Harrison.

Alex perched on the arm of Chiverton's chair and put an arm round his shoulders, the long gaze exchanged by them an affectionate one. This tavern was one of the few places where they could be openly fond of each other. The problem was less the unlikely possibility that people would discern their relationship and more that people would be appalled at the friendship between an upper-class man and working class actor. "This is a pleasant surprise."

"Mr MacPherson!" Mr Fillinister exclaimed at the same time from another direction. He hurried over to their group, expression eager. "How is your crime inquiry progressing?"

"It is still too early to have any definite answers, but I promise you that we are doing all we can. We have found out a lot about the duke's life and acquaintances and hope to soon find something that will prove Miss McNeil's innocence."

"Did you hear that they sent the King's Messenger himself to hunt her down?" Alex said to Ewan. "The bastards haven't spoken to any of us, nor conducted any investigation themselves, but they're still determined to arrest and hang her."

Mr Fillinister looked beseechingly at Ewan, who said, "We will do everything possible to prevent that." He hoped his words were not a lie. He was still not certain that Miss McNeil had not committed the crime. As Alex struck up a humorous tale that kept the rest of the group entertained, Ewan said to Mr Fillinister, "Would you answer an odd question and tell me if Tim Harrison is courting anyone at present?"

"Oh, you heard of his affair with Kenina," Fillinister correctly guessed. "No, there's no reason to think he might have killed Raden.

He was the one who ended things with Kenina, although it did upset him when she first got involved with the duke. I think he realised then what he had lost. He probably also felt guilty at his own behaviour and wanted to make sure she wasn't hurt a second time. Wealthy men often develop a fondness for actresses, but they don't always treat them well."

"Someone recently said that the duke did not take his responsibilities seriously. Do you think he might have been about to let down Miss McNeil?"

Fillinister hesitated then said, "They loved each other. Who knows what might have happened in the future, but I've got no doubt of the truth of that."

Ewan wondered what had made the man pause before speaking, what he was holding back, but applause sounded at the end of Alex's tale, so he could no longer talk privately to Fillinister. He ordered a round of drinks for the group.

An hour later they were all talking merrily when a man came into the room and approached Fillinister. They spoke privately for a moment and then the man left. Fillinister leaned a hand against the wall of the tavern, head bent over.

"Joe, what's wrong?" Alex called to him.

Fillinister turned back towards them and Ewan saw that there were tears in his eyes. "They've got her. They've caught Kenina."

19. CONVERSATION IN OLD TOLBOOTH GAOL

ISHBEL RECEIVED the note from Mr MacPherson, sent late the previous night after she was already asleep, from her lady's maid when she woke up. When she saw what was written, she sat up and pulled back the bed covers.

"Lucy, would you get my clothes and help me dress at once?"

"Is something wrong, miss?"

Ishbel took off her nightgown and hurriedly washed her body in the freezing water from the wash basin, ignoring Lucy's protest about bringing up hot water.

"Miss McNeil has been arrested and taken to the Old Tolbooth gaol. Mr MacPherson and I must see her immediately."

She dried herself and then Lucy laced Ishbel into her stays, then added petticoats and woollen waistcoat.

Lucy held up a pretty blue robe à la polonaise, but Ishbel said, "No, I had better wear one of my oldest gowns. I doubt the conditions at the gaol will be ideal."

Lucy did as she asked but said, "Must you visit such a place? It'll give you nightmares. Couldn't Mr MacPherson go alone this once?"

"Miss McNeil is the most important person in this business," Ishbel said, lifting her arms so Lucy could help her into the dress, then use ribbons to loop the sides of the skirts up, creating the necessary fullness in the panels that modern fashion demanded. "I need to see for myself what kind of woman she is, to know if she is capable of having committed such a terrible crime herself. If not, then she is the best person to tell us who else might have killed the duke."

She penned a brief letter to Mr MacPherson to let him know that she was available as soon as he was ready to visit the gaol, giving it to a footman to take to him as she came downstairs. Breakfast was not usually served for another half hour so the dining room was empty, but another footman took her verbal apology to the kitchen staff and request for any food that could be quickly prepared. Within minutes, plates and cutlery were being placed on the table at her place and her morning drink of chocolate was being brought in, soon followed by fresh bread with butter and jam.

Mr MacPherson arrived as she was finishing and bowed as he said, "Mr Fillinister will meet us at the gaol to make the introduction and so he can see Miss McNeil. He tried to visit her last night, but the guards would not allow him access. I have brought with me a suitable sum of money to ensure we can speak to her."

They walked out into the hall. "A bribe?"

"It might not be necessary," he said, "but I do not want to lose our chance. The case involves the murder of a member of the peerage, so I imagine an early date will be set for the trial, perhaps as little as a fortnight from now."

"Then the crime must be solved as swiftly as possible," she said, accepting her mantelet from Lucy and putting it over her shoulders, then tying it with ribbons. She then took her broad-brimmed hat and gloves, donning these. "I hope Miss McNeil has some idea of who the killer could be or, at least, can reduce our list of suspects."

"I can also help with that," Mr MacPherson said, as Gallach opened the front door for them and they ventured out into temperatures so cold that her breath left a mist in the air. He told her what he had learnt about Tim Harrison as they set out in his carriage for the gaol.

Mr Fillinister was waiting for them at the entrance to the building, arms clasped round his body and features pinched with cold. She stood with him as Mr MacPherson spoke to a guard and handed him a number of guineas. The guard then led them inside.

The stench in the building was almost overpowering and caused all three of them to reach for kerchiefs to place over their noses. Ishbel wished she had thought to soak the cloth in fragrance to cloak the odour, afraid it might cause her to vomit.

They followed the guard into an even more foul-smelling part of the building, grateful for the lantern he held that lit up the semi-dark interior, and he unlocked a door for them.

"Joe!" the woman inside exclaimed, hurrying forward.

As the two of them embraced, Ishbel looked round the cell. There was nothing more than straw to sit or lie on and a chamber pot in the far corner contributed to the stench.

Mr Fillinister introduced Miss McNeil to them and explained to her how they came to be working to free her.

"I am so grateful to you both," she said, wiping tears from her cheeks. Ishbel could see that her features would normally be lovely but, hidden beneath the grime accumulated from a week on the run and drawn from cold and hunger, Miss McNeil looked haggard and exhausted. Her brown hair had fallen out of its clasp and her blue eyes were dull. "I wish I could at least offer you a chair to sit in."

"It is not important," Mr MacPherson said, giving her a kind smile.

"I fear we have little time left to prove your innocence," Ishbel said to her. "Are you strong enough to answer a number of questions?"

"Yes, of course. Anything."

"I hope you will forgive me," Mr MacPherson said, "but this must be asked before we can proceed. Did you kill the Duke of Raden?"

Miss McNeil looked him in the eye and said, "No."

There was nothing shifty about her reaction, only a definite response, and Ishbel believed her. "Could you tell us everything you remember from the night he died and the morning after it?"

"There is little to tell." Miss McNeil leaned against the stone wall of the cell, clearly almost too worn out to remain upright. "I wish I knew more – I wish it desperately – but I knew nothing of the duke's arrival at my house. I had hoped he would visit me that evening and was feeling disappointed that there was no sign of him as I went to bed. At an early hour I was woken by a maid saying my name urgently. She said he was dead. I couldn't take it in. I ran downstairs and when I saw him there, lying in a pool of blood..."

She paled and Mr Fillinister hurried forward to put an arm around her.

Mr MacPherson spoke to the guard, placing another coin in his hand as he asked for a hot drink to be brought. She then heard the guard call to someone else to watch over the unlocked room while he left.

"Forgive me," Miss McNeil said, straightening and taking in several steadying breaths. "I am well, but you can't imagine the nightmare I've lived in since that awful morning. I can answer more questions."

"Why did you leave?" Ishbel asked.

"My first thought was to send for a doctor, but it was clearly far too late for anyone to help poor Richard. The housekeeper was asking me what to do, but I couldn't think, couldn't tear my eyes away from his dead body. I can't say how many minutes passed. I asked who had done this and she said she didn't know, that no one had opened the door to him the previous night, nor heard any noises, and no one had broken a window or door to force their way in. It then struck me that others would assume I'd killed him: he was in my house after all and no other visitor was there. I could think of no way to prove my innocence. I told them that I had to leave or I'd be arrested and said that they should wait several hours, then send for the Town Guards. I ran upstairs, dressed, packed a handful of clothes and ran. I went to Joe first, telling him what had happened, and he gave me all the money on him and said I should take a coach to London and try to get passage on a ship out of the country. I got as far as London, but I had too little money left to proceed further. I thought I could remain there until the real murderer was found, but an officer found and arrested me, bringing me back."

"When you left your house, did you see any knife that could have been used to commit the crime?" Mr MacPherson asked her.

"No, I..."

There was a sound behind them and they turned as the guard entered the room and handed Miss McNeil a drink in a crude tankard and a lump of bread. She thanked him gratefully, not seeming to realise that this was no kindness on his part but the work of Mr MacPherson's bribe. She took several swallows of the hot drink, whatever it was, which seemed to revive her.

"A knife? Do you mean beside Richard's body?" she asked Mr MacPherson, who nodded. "I saw nothing. There were knives in the kitchen."

"None of them were used," he told her. "We also saw a letter opener that could perhaps have been used, but there was no blood on it."

"Then the killer must have brought a knife with him?" she mused, finishing her drink. "Many people carry a folding knife for protection. I do. It was with my clothes the morning after the death, so no one used that."

"It is not something a gentleman would commonly carry," Mr MacPherson said, with a glance at Ishbel. There was a moment of silence as they all considered this information, then he asked Miss McNeil, "Do you have any idea who the killer could be?"

"I had two thoughts about it, firstly that a thief somehow had a key to my door, although I cannot imagine how. My second belief, which seemed more probable, was that Lord Moray had done it. He was a friend of Richard's..."

"We know," Ishbel said. "We have met him. Do you know what their disagreement was about?"

Miss McNeil finished chewing a piece of bread before speaking, the expression of hunger on her face making Ishbel think she had not had much, or perhaps any food recently. "Richard suggested that they invest in some venture and it lost a great deal of money. I think Lord Moray had put even more money into it than Richard had and felt that Richard should pay him back himself. Richard refused, saying he had known the risk. They argued and had still not reconciled when Richard was murdered. Richard said something about Lord Moray not being trustworthy around women too – I think he must have heard some of the crude comments Lord Moray made to me. He wanted to protect me." She put the tankard down on the floor and straightened, taking a step closer to them. "What I thought was that, unless someone else had obtained a key somehow, Richard must have arrived with his murderer, meaning that it was someone he knew and felt safe to let into the house. I thought there could have been another argument between the two men and Lord Moray lost his temper – he has a really nasty temper – and stabbed him. However, as you say, most gentlemen do not need to keep a knife on them. Could he have used my letter opener and then wiped it clean?"

"That is possible," Mr MacPherson said.

"Our other main suspect is the duke's daughter," Ishbel told her.

"Lady Sarah? Why would you possibly believe such a thing?"

"She seemed to have a bad relationship with her father and has inherited a great deal of money on his death. There was also a rumour that you and the duke might marry, which would make her fear losing her inheritance to you and any male heir you produced."

"No, Richard was never going to marry me," Miss McNeil said and gave a quick laugh, a painful sound. "Can you imagine me attending some fancy ball with him and mixing with the gentry? They would have destroyed me if I'd done such a thing. He gave me a good life: his affection, a lovely home and more money and gifts than I ever expected. Why should I ask for more than that?"

"Lady Sarah might not have realised you felt like that. She is the only other person we have heard of with a motive to kill the duke," Ishbel said. "She could have asked a servant or admirer to commit the murder on her behalf, which would explain them taking a knife with them, and there would have been no reason for the duke to feel threatened by such a visitor, so he would have let them into the house."

"How horrible. It never occurred to me to suspect his own daughter could think of such a thing, but if you believe it possible then so do I. How will you prove it?"

That was, unfortunately, a question they had no good answer for.

20. TIME RUNNING OUT

IT WAS still early morning when they left the Old Tolbooth, taking their leave of Miss McNeil and Mr Fillinister. They returned to Miss Campbell's house to talk over what they had learnt. Ewan had left some money with a guard so he would provide Miss McNeil with a blanket and decent food and drink.

They settled themselves in the library, its fire hot and servants close by to provide them with refreshments, and Ewan could not help but compare it to the hellish place they had just been and to the luxurious life he usually took for granted.

"I cannot believe anyone could be kept in such appalling conditions," Miss Campbell said, echoing his thoughts. "Miss McNeil has not even had a trial yet and such treatment must kill many of its inmates. I must ask Harriette if there is any charitable society that might be able to improve matters for prisoners."

"If there is, I would be glad to contribute to it," Ewan said, grabbing this idea as a salve to his conscience at having so much wealth.

"I believe more than ever that Miss McNeil is innocent. Do you have any doubts about her?"

"She was convincing but do not forget that she is an actress. I would certainly not consider her one of the most likely suspects, but I am not yet ready to absolve her of the crime."

"Our two best suspects must remain Lady Sarah and Lord Moray."

"Yes," he said, a picture coming to his mind of the cold anger on Lady Sarah's face as she spoke of her father. "Perhaps I should send Rabbie for another talk with Lady Sarah's servants."

"Certainly. And perhaps Mr Cassell – the caddie who helped us before – could ask around about the two of them amongst his acquaintances. He might even be able to find someone who saw who entered Miss McNeil's house on the night the duke died." When Ewan agreed with this, she went on, "I will send for him while you speak to your valet."

Ewan felt this was not entirely proper, but the young Highlander had been nothing but polite to Miss Campbell in the past, and he doubted she would listen to his objection in any case, so he agreed to speak to her tomorrow. She had several university lectures she wished to attend this afternoon, and this would give Rabbie and Jed Cassell a chance to find out what they could.

He left the house, still lost in thought about the case. It seemed most probable to him that Lord Moray was the killer, but a confident gentleman like that would not be likely to make a confession of his guilt if they confronted him. He said this to Rabbie, as he requested his help and changed out of the malodorous outfit he had worn to the gaol, feeling a bit guilty as he saw his valet's downcast expression at the state of the soiled clothes.

"A jury would never even consider a peer of the realm as the murderer when they have an easier person to blame in Miss McNeil. We need evidence of his guilt."

"Best to be sure you're accusing the right person of murder before you worry about that, if you'll pardon me for saying so, sir," Rabbie said, tying a fresh cravat around Ewan's neck.

"No, you're right, but between you and Jed, the caddie, I hope you can get enough information to let us be certain of the culprit. We are rapidly running out of time. If the trial begins before we have another good suspect to put before a jury, Miss McNeil could hang..."

21. THOUGHTS ABOUT THE KILLER

MR MACPHERSON brought his valet with him when he called at Ishbel's home the next day.

"I could not find much out that you do not already know," Rabbie Camran said, sitting carefully on the edge of a chair in the drawing room in worn but well-maintained clothes. His sharp features were full of enthusiasm and, as before, he spoke with a familiarity to Mr MacPherson that suggested a friendship between them, despite their different stations in life. "Lady Sarah seemed to strongly dislike her father, but they knew of no man who she might take into her confidence. I was thinking about what Mr MacPherson said to me yesterday about someone killing the duke for her. It didn't seem as if any of the servants liked her and, if there wasn't no other man she trusted, who does that leave?"

"That is a good discovery," she told him.

"There's a chance I can find out more," he said eagerly. "A footman mentioned that today Lady Sarah's maid has the afternoon off so, if you both think it's a good idea, I could try to have a private talk with her and perhaps offer her a bit of money to tell us what she knows. If there is anyone who would know all Lady Sarah's secrets, it's her lady's maid."

"I agree," Mr MacPherson said and they both looked to her for approval.

"So do I. You are doing a wonderful job of helping us, Mr Camran."

The valet grinned, clearly enjoying playing his part in their investigation. It seemed as if it was not just she and Mr MacPherson who were stepping outside their usual roles in life and relishing the change.

"Rabbie," Mr MacPherson said, "see if the maid saw any blood, either on Lady Sarah or any possible accomplice. I cannot believe the murder could have been committed without blood getting on the killer's clothes and that would be a clear sign of guilt we could put before a jury."

"Yes, sir."

When the valet left them, Mr MacPherson asked, "Did you manage to speak to Jed Cassell yesterday?"

"Yes. He already knew Lord Moray and seemed unsurprised at the thought that he might be a killer," she told him, Mr Cassell's information having sealed her dislike of Lord Moray. "Apparently, the lord's show of good manners does not extend to his servants or to other working-class people he encounters. He once punched his valet while drunk and frequently has affairs with the maids who work in his house, several having left to escape his attentions."

"We have been told by more than one person that he has a bad temper. If he was drunk when he turned up at Duke Raden's house, it is highly probable that he killed him in a fit of rage."

She frowned, not seeing how this would fit with the events of the night. "Where did he get a knife from?"

"The letter opener could have been used."

"And, drunk, having just killed a friend, he thought to wipe it clean of blood? Why would he even bother? It would not link him to the crime in any way."

Ewan leaned back in his armchair, silent, a considering frown on his expressive face. "You are right. It does not make sense."

"There is still Lady Sarah to consider."

"But if she did not know about Miss McNeil until after her father was dead, she has little motive."

"Perhaps she found out about her that very night and, in a burst of anger at the thought of such a liaison tainting her family's name or of her father begetting a male heir who would disinherit her, she arranged the murder – or committed it herself – straight away."

"That is possible."

She could tell he was not convinced. They would have to wait – impatiently in her case – and hope that Mr Camran and Mr Cassell found out what they needed to be sure of the killer. With Miss McNeil awaiting trial, they had to solve the murder quickly.

22. POSSIBLE KILLERS

WHILE THE valet and caddie searched for proof of the killer on their behalf, Ishbel attended another informal luncheon with her cousin. She had attempted to avoid it but, of course, Harriette would not countenance that, saying Ishbel must be seen in society as soon as possible after being publicly insulted, to show that she was not cowed by the words. This was not entirely true. Ishbel was terrified of another such scene, her usual sense of independence and indifference to the opinions of the highest level of society vanishing when confronted with such malice.

Upon their arrival their hostess, Mrs Gleeson, greeted them. She was an unusually tall lady in a green gown that had the unfortunate effect of turning her complexion slightly sallow. She spoke to them in a friendly manner, but Ishbel was sure she caught a note of contempt in her voice.

Harriette was immediately seized upon to give her opinion on some matter, so Ishbel was left alone amid the roomful of guests. They were in the elegant formal dining room of Mrs Gleeson's large city house, which had walls that were half panelled and half decorated with gold and blue striped wallpaper, and mahogany furniture. The dining table had been moved to one end and covered with refreshments, with a footman waiting there to serve the guests, who were standing about in half a dozen groups, the air filled with numerous conversations. Several women glanced in Ishbel's direction and then one of them said something that had them all laughing.

"Miss Campbell!"

Ishbel turned, not recognising the voice and looking about with apprehension, but then she gave a smile of relief and pleasure at seeing the familiar, attractive features of the young lady approaching her. "Miss Chiverton, I am happy to see you again."

"And I, you." Mr Chiverton's sister was wearing a cream gown covered in lace that suited her blonde hair and pale complexion, while making her blue eyes look more vivid than ever. Ishbel had no doubt that she would have plenty of men competing for her affections after her coming-out ball. Miss Chiverton gave Ishbel a bright smile. "How is your murder case proceeding?"

"Well, I think. We hope to be sure of the killer soon; we must be since Miss McNeil, the woman accused of the crime, has now been arrested and will shortly be put on trial."

"Then you will save an innocent woman?"

"I very much hope so." Ishbel glanced round the room. "Is your brother here with you?"

"Not today. My father accompanied me."

"And is your mother recovered from her recent illness?"

"Nearly." The smile returned. "She is still regaining her strength, but the darkest times are over and she will soon be fully restored to health. At her insistence, we have set a date for my coming-out ball, so I may soon attend larger gatherings."

Ishbel failed to see why this was a good thing, but she kept the thought to herself in the face of the young woman's excitement.

"Fiona!" A distinguished-looking, blond-haired gentleman, presumably her father, gestured for Miss Chiverton to join him, glaring at Ishbel.

"Oh, dear! I am so sorry, but I was not supposed to speak to you."

"Because of the scandal now attached to my name," Ishbel guessed at once, trying to hide her disappointment.

"My brother, Eddie, disagreed with the decision, but my parents would not be swayed."

Her father called out to her once again, in a more brusque tone.

"I understand," Ishbel said. "It does not matter. You must go: I do not want you to be scolded because of me."

Miss Chiverton put a hand on Ishbel's arm. "I hope you will still consider me a friend."

"Gladly."

The young woman reluctantly left, returning to her father, who took her to one side, to speak in a way that left her looking downcast, cheeks crimson.

This was Ishbel's fault, her presence now an embarrassment to anyone who associated with her.

Mr MacPherson was waiting with both his valet and Mr Cassell, the caddie, when she got back to the Huntly residence. Harriette took one look at her three callers and, with a long-suffering sigh, invited herself into their meeting as Ishbel's chaperone. Torn between amusement and chagrin, Ishbel silently acknowledged Harriette's right to act in this way – given the repercussions she had recently discovered of being considered unladylike by society.

They all took seats in the library, the working-class men looking thoroughly intimidated by Harriette's presence, their eyes frequently darting over to her silent frowning form.

"What have you discovered?" Ishbel asked them.

All three men exchanged looks, then Rabbie Camran said, "They didn't do it, miss. Neither of them."

"What?" She could not believe it possible, not with all they had learnt. This would destroy their entire research, if true. "How can you be sure of that?"

"It's a delicate matter, Miss Campbell," Mr Cassell said, flushing. "Lady Sarah was seen leaving her house on the night her father died. She spent the night with a male acquaintance... With Lord Moray."

"Good lord!" Harriette exclaimed, expression more intrigued than shocked. "I never would have expected you to say that of Lady Sarah."

For a moment Ishbel did not understand, the words remaining a blank to her, then the implication sank in: Lord Moray and Lady Sarah were having an affair. If they had spent the whole night together, neither of them could be the killer. "No wonder the duke told Miss McNeil that Lord Moray could not be trusted around women. It was not her he was trying to keep out of Lord Moray's sights; it was his daughter!" She tried to clutch at the dissolving findings. "Are you absolutely certain of this information?"

"I'm afraid so, miss," Mr Cassell said. "They were both at Lord Moray's house when the duke was being killed."

She sat still, taking in this blow.

"And now," Mr MacPherson said grimly, "we are down from two

possible killers to none."

"One," she corrected him, although she hated to say it. Four sets of eyes fixed upon her with interest. "We are unfortunately left with the person we never wanted to suspect: Miss McNeil."

23. DEAD END

SILENCE FOLLOWED Ishbel's words, then Harriette said, "Do you mean that the two of you put us all through such a scandalous business for no reason? The Town Guards were right all along, and that must be the first time those words were ever uttered!"

"There must be other possibilities," Mr MacPherson said, getting to his feet and pacing to the library window then back again. "We accepted that Lady Sarah and Lord Moray were the most obvious suspects, so we looked no further."

"We wondered briefly if someone in love with Miss McNeil might have killed the duke, but Tim Harrison, the man she was previously close to, was proven to have no motive. There might be someone else who loves her."

"Joe Fillinister has always shown great affection for her." Although the fact he was the one who had asked them to take on the case made him an improbable suspect. At the moment, though, she would consider anything.

"That is not possible." Mr MacPherson looked uncomfortably at Harriette, who raised an eyebrow at him, then he said to Ishbel, "Joe is of the same nature as... others we know who will never marry."

"You two, out!" Harriette snapped at the unfortunate valet and caddie. Mr MacPherson managed to pay Mr Cassell for his help and then the men fled. Harriette then rounded on the two people who remained. "It astonishes me to learn that you would speak of such matters with each other, let alone that you would let yourselves be overheard by common men who could repeat your conversation to countless others!"

"I trust my valet's discretion entirely," Mr MacPherson said in a stiff, offended tone, "and we have no reason to doubt that Jed Cassell's sole wish is to help us catch a murderer."

"Just the same, you forget yourself in speaking of such things to my unmarried cousin."

Ishbel responded to this: "I insisted some time ago that Mr MacPherson keep no secrets from me during inquiries into criminal matters, no matter how forbidden the subject might usually be. We spoke about such feelings because it was necessary to our search for the killer."

"Hmm." Harriette's expression remained severe. "I suppose I will have to trust you to find more appropriate matters to converse about in my absence."

She got to her feet, shook out the skirts of her gown, glared at them both, and then marched from the room.

"Forgive me. I should not have spoken about the subject in front of your cousin," Mr MacPherson said.

"We must speak of anything we need to in order to get this murder solved," Ishbel answered. "I think we should talk immediately to Mr Fillinister, to find out if we could all be mistaken about Miss McNeil's innocence."

"He will probably be at the theatre at this time." He got to his feet and she followed him into the crisp air outside. When they were seated in his carriage, the vehicle heading to its new destination, he said, "I do not know if any of this is useful now, but Rabbie learned from the lady's maid that the Duke of Raden found out that Lord Moray was courting his daughter and had a terrible argument with her."

Clinging to one final hope on the matter, Ishbel said, "Could Lord Moray and Lady Sarah not have slipped out of his house to kill the duke? This does, after all, give them both an extra reason to commit murder."

"I am afraid there is no possibility left of their guilt. Jed spoke to someone – a woman living on the streets – who saw Lady Sarah arrive at the house in the middle of the night and leave again before dawn, both she and Lord Moray visible to the woman."

"They could still have hired someone to commit the crime."

"Jed thought of that. None of Lord Moray's servants left the house in the night and none of Lady Sarah's servants liked her enough to do such a thing for her. She certainly could not have got a suitor to have acted for her and put herself in his debt, given her relationship with Lord Moray. Jed even asked amongst the criminal classes if Lord Moray had put out word of illegal work he needed someone for, but this never took place."

Then they really were innocent. What an infuriating thing, Ishbel thought, that they should both have the characters of murderers, when neither of them were.

They arrived at the theatre, where scenes were being rehearsed on stage by several actors in front of the empty rows of seats. Mr Fillinister immediately approached them, his hopeful face reminding Ishbel of everything he had done to try to prove his friend's innocence. He took them to an empty dressing room where they could speak privately, closing the door behind them.

"The two people we were looking into are innocent of the murder," Mr MacPherson told him and Mr Fillinister face crumpled.

"Have you no one else to consider?"

"Not that we can think of."

"A suspicion is all we need," Mr Fillinister insisted, a hand on Mr MacPherson's arm as he entreated them both. "Just enough to convince a jury that there were others with a better motive than Kenina who could've killed the duke."

Ishbel, sitting in the room's only chair, leaned towards him. "Is it possible you were wrong? Could Miss McNeil be the guilty person?"

"No," he said without hesitation. "I've known her for longer than anyone else and I swear to you that she couldn't have done this. She's innocent – you have to believe that."

She and Mr MacPherson looked at each other and, believing Mr Fillinister's certainty, Ishbel nodded.

"All right," Mr MacPherson said, "then we must start again and find other suspects. You told me that Tim Harrison was not still in love with her, but could any of the other actors have such feelings?"

"No. Two members of the troupe are married to each other; two more are having an affair; Alex and I are incapable of that kind of love for a woman. The others are too new to the group to have formed such an attachment and, in any case, never showed a partiality to Kenina. There's no one here to suspect. It must be someone connected with the duke."

"Then we will find them," Mr MacPherson said firmly.

"The courts have set the trial date," Mr Fillinister told them.

"Already?" she exclaimed, horrified. "When?"

"The fourteenth day of December. Less than three weeks."

"We will do all we can," Ishbel told him, but his eyes remained bleak, haunting her after she and Mr MacPherson left him in the empty room.

24. A FRESH PATH TO FOLLOW

EDDIE'S MOTHER was feeling sufficiently strong to join the family at the dinner table that night for the first time since she became ill, which gave the gathering a happier atmosphere than it had had in years and managed to put a smile on even his brother's face. They discussed Fiona's coming-out ball, his mother and sister lit up with pleasure at the opportunity to make plans for the event, instead of having their decisions made for them. Eddie hoped Fiona would exercise her usual good sense while being courted and would not hurry into marriage in a desire to escape the restrictions of her current life.

They were all in the drawing room when the butler announced Mr MacPherson's unexpected arrival. Eddie left them to go and greet his friend, who reluctantly gave his greatcoat to the butler, face pinched with cold, as he said, "I was hoping you would be willing to give me a fresh opinion on this business with the Duke of Raden."

Pleased to be trusted with this, Eddie took him into the gaming room and fixed them both a glass of whiskey, while Ewan told him the events of the day. Eddie listened intently and sympathised over their inquiry leading nowhere.

"We must learn all we can about the duke," MacPherson said, sitting opposite him, a cards table beside them, "in the hope that this will show us the killer's identity."

"Had he no one at all but his daughter to inherit his estate?" Eddie asked, absently shuffling a pack of cards. "No distant relative?"

"There was no such person at his funeral service or wake and, of course, we cannot ask Lady Sarah, when she knows we suspected her."

"He was such a likeable man." Eddie turned over the King of Diamonds as he thought over what Alex had told him about Raden.

The duke had sounded more interested in love than power or money and had treated others with kindness. "I find it hard to believe that many people could have had cause to wish him harm."

"Lord Moray said – if anything spoken by him can be believed – that the duke did not take his responsibilities seriously. Who, other than a relative, would he have looked after? Servants? No, Rabbie said they had liked their master. Could he have had another mistress before he met Miss McNeil?"

"Bound to, I should imagine, and a spurned lover's fury seems more likely to me than anything else, given what I know of him."

"It is certainly a possibility." MacPherson looked cheered by the idea.

"Let me ask about," Eddie said. "People are less suspicious of me these days, now that they know what you are up to."

MacPherson nodded and gave a smile. "Thank you."

Eddie summoned a carriage as MacPherson's rattled away, quickly changed his outfit and travelled to a club that was popular with the highest levels of male society. As he bought himself a drink – surrounded by the smell of alcohol and tobacco, the sound of conversations and men making bets on cards and dice – he wondered who would be the best person to approach. He needed a gentleman who would know all the gossip about a duke and would not immediately discern that Eddie was acting on MacPherson's behalf.

His gaze settled on Lord Bentley, the young heir to the Wutherham estate, who was hovering nervously around an older group, who were playing dice. His family had influential friends, but the lad did not mix in the same circles as Eddie's friends, he himself only receiving an introduction through a casual acquaintance.

He walked across the room, greeting several people as he did so, and clapped the boy on the back. "Lord Bentley, I haven't seen you in months. How are you?"

The boy turned, brightening at the attention. "Never better, Mr Chiverton. Yourself?"

"Having been discussing the Duke of Raden's death with a friend, I am feeling the fragility of life and am, therefore, in great need of a drink." He held up his glass as he spoke and Bentley smiled.

"Has a date been set for the trial of the duke's killer, do you know?"

"His mistress, you mean? The current one, at least. I believe the trial will take place in December, although there are rumours that others had a better motive than she for the murder. You might have heard more than I on the subject, your family being so well connected."

Bentley leaned slightly nearer to say, "The Duke of Raden was known to have a great affection for ladies of all types, both during his marriage and after his wife's death."

"I wondered if he might have left a previous mistress when he courted the actress, someone who might have killed him in a fit of jealous passion."

"I hope not. My brother's friend's cousin, Lord Asquith, is actually in contact – romantically speaking – with the Lady of the Night Raden used to visit." Bentley gestured to the gentleman who was reclining in a chair, legs stretched out and crossed at the ankles, ready to trip up anyone blinded by the tobacco smoke.

Eddie smiled as he took another sip of his wine. "How interesting."

25. THE DUKE'S AFFAIRS

EWAN CALLED upon Lady Morrelly, his aunt, the next morning. She had the footman show him into her sewing room, where she sat with a piece of embroidery he had seen half-completed for at least the past five years. On a chair beside her sat Aloysius, her cat, who was staring fixedly into the left-hand corner of the room. Ewan instinctively followed the cat's gaze but could see nothing there other than the brightly striped wallpaper.

He kissed his aunt and sat in a damask-upholstered chair opposite her.

After asking about her health and Aloysius's health, he said, "I wondered what you could tell me about the Duke of Raden. Anything you know."

"His daughter is of marriageable age," she said at once, predictably. She had been requesting to be told of his upcoming nuptials since he turned sixteen.

"Anything else?"

She sighed in disappointment at his lack of helpfulness in her marital plans for him. "We were all awaiting the announcement of the duke's marriage, until his untimely death ruined Rachel's dreams."

"Rachel?" he asked, confused.

"Mrs Rachel Ainsley is the widowed lady he had been showing a marked interest in, although his attentions were less clear in recent months."

When he fell for Miss MacNeil, presumably. "Was Mrs Ainsley annoyed at his apparent change of heart?"

"She believed, as we all did, that he was simply busy of late. She is a wealthy lady from an excellent family, who developed a clear liking for him. He would have been a fool to turn away from such a match."

Indeed! And how would Mrs Ainsley have felt if she knew she had been replaced in his affections by a working-class actress?

"Meeow!" said Aloysius loudly, standing up and staring over Ewan's shoulder into the left corner.

Ewan jumped and looked sharply behind him. The fact he could see nothing there somehow made Aloysius's focus more, rather than less, disturbing.

His aunt looked up from her embroidery. "You seem a little nervous today, dear."

Ewan called upon Miss Campbell after seeing his aunt. She was in the drawing room with Lady Huntly, who looked at Ewan as though he was a disobedient child in need of a scolding.

"Your footman left that for you," Lady Huntly said, gesturing with her fan towards a letter with a seal on it that he instantly recognised. "Apparently you are now so frequent a visitor that your staff is under the impression you are living here."

"My apologies for any inconvenience," he said, ripping the seal and unfolding the letter. He quickly read through it. "It seems as if we have two more possible murder suspects to consider."

"How wonderful," Lady Huntly responded, her tone dripping sarcasm. "You can find ways to scandalise Edinburgh society even further."

"Perhaps we should talk in the library," Miss Campbell suggested with a meaningful look at her cousin that the lady ignored.

"If you wish," he replied willingly.

They left Lady Huntly to find someone else to insult and took their usual seats in the large room, then Ewan told her what his visit to his aunt had revealed.

"I believe I met Mrs Ainsley at a musical evening some time ago," Miss Campbell said. "She certainly seemed a determined lady and for the duke to have publicly courted her and then not carried through and proposed would have been deeply embarrassing. Did the letter tell you something more?"

"It was from Chiverton. I spoke to him last night and he said he would ask questions about the duke on my behalf, believing people might be more open with him now that our investigation is generally known. We wondered if the duke might have had a mistress before

Miss McNeil, whom he cast aside when he met her, and that seems to have been the case."

"Did he find out her name?"

"Yes: Cathy Smith. However, he says she is not believed to be in the least respectable, moving from one man to another. I know you do not pay attention to such things, but perhaps I should speak to her alone – your reputation has suffered enough over this case and also I do not wish to cause any further problems between you and Lady Huntly."

She hesitated, biting her lip, and he wished he could find a way to make her life easier. She was good at this work, but everyone was treating her as if she was behaving in an immoral manner, which was opposite of the truth.

If she would agree to marry him, society would be more tolerant. For a moment he almost did repeat his offer of marriage: he loved and admired her so much; just the sight of her face always lifted his mood. She would never accept a proposal for such a reason as respectability, though, and would he really want her to? No, he wished for her to return his feelings to the point that she wanted more than anything to marry him, and he was not sure that that would ever be true.

"Very well," she said at last.

His heart stuttered, having lost what question she was answering and been lost in his own dreams. Then he realised what she was talking about and disappointment ran through him.

He bowed and left her.

26. AN UGLY ENCOUNTER

ISHBEL WAS annoyed with herself for letting Mr MacPherson go alone to speak to the duke's former acquaintance. She had given in and behaved as society would have wanted and she hated the thought of one day giving up all work, this and her university studies, out of fear of society's censure. She would not let herself be cowed again.

She went to speak to Harriette, having to wait until her cousin had finished speaking to the French chef about the menu for an upcoming dinner party she was holding.

When the man had left, his expression peeved, Ishbel said, "Do you know where I might encounter Mrs Ainsley today?"

"She is not a particular acquaintance of mine and I do not often see her at the entertainments I am invited to, but I believe she has a weakness for anything of a musical nature. You might find her at Sir Andrew Middleton's gathering this afternoon, as he has a renowned pianist playing there. I can obtain an invitation for you but I have a charitable meeting I need to attend and Lord Huntly will be delivering a lecture at the College, so you would have to go alone."

Ishbel ignored the stab of fear at the thought of enduring insulting comments with no one to stand at her side. She could do this; she was not weak. "Thank you, I will."

Four hours later she was dressed in one of her finest gowns, hair curled and puffed out at the sides, walking into the home of Sir Andrew Middleton. A couple of dozen people were already there: women with faces painted white and a dab of red at their cheeks, wearing grand silk gowns and men in brightly coloured breeches, waistcoats and jackets, elaborate neckcloths and white wigs. Ishbel looked round for a familiar face, finally seeing only someone she would rather avoid: Lord Moray. However, he would very likely be acquainted with Mrs Ainsley and could tell Ishbel if the lady was here.

He was amongst a group of half a dozen people, many ladies included, so it was not improper for her to join them.

She did so, giving an uncomfortable smile to the several women her own age who looked at her with curiosity. Lord Moray caught sight of her and gave a bow. "How beautiful you look, Miss Campbell," he said with a roguish smile. "I am quite transfixed."

She gave a quick curtsy, wondering if he gave the same compliments to Lady Sarah. No wonder the duke had wanted to keep the two of them apart. "It is a pleasure to see you again, Lord Moray. Is Mrs Ainsley with your party? I had hoped to speak with her today."

"I believe I saw her a short time ago," another young man said, whom Lord Moray introduced as Mr Hannam. "Please allow me to escort you to her."

"Thank you." She took his arm and he walked her to a different part of the room and then paused, looking about. Ishbel had only a faint recollection of the lady's appearance, so she had to rely on his knowledge.

"Ah, there she is." He walked confidently to open doors that led out to the garden. She hesitated, pulling her hand free of his arm. "Did you not wish to see Mrs Ainsley after all?" he asked in a confused tone.

She looked beyond him. There were a few people outside and she did not want to miss this chance to progress the investigation. "Yes."

They moved through the doorway, out of sight of the others, and then he grabbed her arms and dragged her to one side. It was as if he had turned into something inhuman. He pushed her roughly against the side of the house and leaded forward, his lips seeking hers. Panicking, she turned her head from the kiss and tried to pull away, struggling with him, but he held her arms in an immovable grip.

His mouth touched hers, damp and insistent, and she kicked him in the shins as hard as she could.

He swore and let her go, and she got free of him. "How dare you!" She backed away and re-entered the drawing room, but he followed her inside.

"Do not affect innocence now," he whispered in a mocking tone, leaning close, as if he might attack her again here, amongst other people. "You knew what I wanted. Lord Moray told me what manner of woman you really are."

She backed away, wanting to slap the smile off his face, but that would only attract attention and cause another scandal. She struggled to take in this unfair excuse, that he apparently felt allowed him to behave in such a way. "You are revolting."

He moved closer and she could not bear the thought of him touching her again. She hurried away through the crowds, not caring how her abrupt departure might look, and ran down the steps of the house to her awaiting carriage. Only when she was safely inside and it was moving towards her home, did she feel out of danger.

She began to shake, her body ice-cold, her breathing uneven.

She had always scorned upper class views on proper behaviour for a lady, but this was what happened when she acted against them. This was what, until now, she had been protected from.

A wave of nausea swept over her and she gripped the seat of the carriage tightly, swallowing down bile.

She wished fervently she had kept to her unconventional but safe university studies and had never got involved in looking into criminal matters.

27. A PAST DALLIANCE

EWAN WAS glad Miss Campbell had remained safely at home instead of accompanying him to a neighbourhood such as this. The street where Cathy Smith lived was utterly different from the respectable one where Miss McNeil's house was situated.

Ewan got out of his carriage and two women at once approached him with fake smiles and partly unbuttoned dresses to ask if he wanted companionship for the evening.

"No, thank you," he told them. His only bedroom experience had been gained with such a woman and, while he did not exactly regret the experience, it was one he felt some shame over. It had not miraculously turned him from boy into man as he had hoped; only time and responsibility had done that. The thought of constantly finding one lover after another, as the duke seemed to have done, held no attraction when compared to the thought of marrying someone he loved and remaining true to her. If she would ever have him.

Waste of every kind littered the pavement and road, and several rats fought over something – he did not want to know what – in a dark corner.

He checked the numbers of the doors and, seeing the one he wanted, knocked upon it. A short while later he heard light steps and a woman opened the door. She was much younger than Miss McNeil, probably little more than twenty, and had a pretty face and full figure. "Yes?" she said to him, a touch wary.

"Miss Smith?" he checked and, when he nodded, said, "I am

looking into the Duke of Raden's murder and hoped to speak briefly to you."

"Aye, all right. You best come inside then." He followed her into a shabby parlour that held only the most basic of furniture and smelt of tallow candles.

"Had you already heard of his death?" he asked as she waved him into a chair and sat down across the room from him.

"Aye. Most people around here knew he called on me for a while – it was him who paid for this house." She looked proud of the fact and, seeing his expression, said, "It might not look much to a gent like you, but I was stuck with my stepdad and nine brothers and sisters. I woulda done anything to get away, but the duke was good to me."

"He treated you kindly?"

"Yes. He was gentle with me and bought me gifts."

"You must have been sorry when he stopped calling on you?" He looked for signs of anger in her but could see none.

"Sure I was. He rented somewhere bigger than this for me at first, but I knew it would end one day. He left me with this house and enough money to make sure I dinna starve. It was more generous than he had to be."

He could see that she meant it. She certainly had no cause to kill him. "Did you have any idea about who might have killed him?"

"The actress he took up with, I heard. A thief or ruffian coulda done it, but wasna he murdered in her house?"

"Miss McNeil has been accused of the crime, but I think she might be innocent."

"Then good luck to the poor lassie. The law don't care what happens to our sort."

With these words in his head, he thanked her for her time with words and a coin and headed back outside into the cold. His coach-driver asked where to take him and Ewan hesitated. He took the pocket watch from his waistcoat pocket and checked the time: mid-afternoon. Miss Campbell would probably be out attending lectures. He would see if Chiverton or McDonald were home and call on Miss Campbell tomorrow.

28. AFTERMATH

ISHBEL HAD avoided speaking to anyone the previous evening by claiming to have a severe headache. It meant she could have no dinner, but the plain scones and fruit Lucy brought her were all she wanted anyway.

She had repeatedly scrubbed her body with soap and water last night and still been unable to rid herself of the feeling of that man's damp mouth pushing against hers; his hands upon her arms.

She had stifled the sound of her sobbing against her pillow, wanting no one, not even Lucy, to know what had happened. It had been all her own fault. She had acted outside the acceptable manner for a lady and men like Hannam would feel justified in attacking her from now on. She might never be safe again.

She washed her face before Lucy arrived and then her maid helped her to dress, donning a woollen waistcoat for warmth beneath the fine wool of her gown.

"Your arm is bruised!" Lucy exclaimed with concern. "How did you do that?"

Ishbel looked down at the large green bruise forming and realised it was the impression of that man's hand, when he had held her so she could not get away from him...

She pulled the gown loose. "I will wear something with long sleeves. It is too cold for this today."

Lucy obeyed, asking no further questions, but it was clear from her expression that she knew something was wrong.

Harriette and Lord Huntly were already sitting at the dining table, eating breakfast, when Ishbel entered the room.

"Are you feeling better today, my dear?" Lord Huntly asked her, lowering his newspaper.

"Yes, I am entirely recovered now, thank you."

"It is not like you to fall ill like that," Harriette said, observing Ishbel with a sharp gaze.

"No. It was strange. Perhaps I ate something in the afternoon that made me unwell."

She helped herself to a light meal, stomach churning at the thought of cooked food. Gallach held out a silver tray with a letter for her and she broke the seal and unfolded it, then could have cried at the contents. If she had wanted to stay out of sight for a while, she was about to be forced to do the opposite.

"What is it?" Harriette asked.

"The date for Viscount Inderly's trial has been fixed for next week and I have been asked to give evidence."

"Good. Then you can soon put the matter behind you."

Ishbel nodded, trying to think of it in this way, when all she wanted to do was lock herself away in her room.

Mr MacPherson was announced as she was about to walk upstairs, so she greeted him, forcing a smile and gestured towards the library.

"I spoke to Cathy Smith yesterday," he said as they entered the library. He put a hand lightly on her arm, something he had done countless times in the past, but her mind instantly recalled the painful grip of that other man. She pulled away from his touch in a panic, breathing quick, shallow breaths, for a moment unable to get enough air into her lungs.

"Miss Campbell, what is wrong?" he asked, hand held out towards her and worry in his eyes. "Please tell me."

She looked down. How could she speak of such a thing? "It is nothing."

"That is clearly untrue."

She swallowed, her throat dry. "When I was at the musical event yesterday a gentleman – hardly a gentleman – tried to kiss me. He said Lord Moray had said..."

"...Said what?" he asked her urgently.

"... That I was the kind of woman he could treat in that way."

"That cad! I will demand satisfaction from him."

A duel? She caught hold of his arm without even thinking about the touch, too concerned with his safety to feel any misgivings over it. "No, you must not. It would... it would only damage my name further." She thought that her reputation could hardly be brought much lower, but knew he would listen to such an appeal.

"I will at least speak to him, warn him from ever speaking of you in such a way again."

"It is not necessary. Do you not see? I flouted society's rules over and over and this was the consequence. It was my own doing."

"It was not!" he exclaimed, his vehement reaction easing her shame. "Your behaviour may be unusual, but it has never been immoral in any way."

"I should have realised his intention in leading me away from the other people."

"A gentleman would never have behaved in such a way."

He truly did not blame her, Ishbel realised. Maybe she had not been at fault. Abruptly, the room lurched and her hands flailed, hitting the wooden floor beneath her.

"Miss Campbell!" Mr MacPherson crouched down in front of her. "Can I get you a glass of water or wine? What can I do?"

"Did I just swoon?" she asked him, confused. "How embarrassing."

He gave a shaky laugh and she realised she had scared him. "It is hardly surprising, given what you endured."

"Miss Campbell!" a footman exclaimed from the doorway and rushing forwards.

"Oh, dear. Calum, you may assist Mr MacPherson in helping me up, but please promise me that you will not inform Lady Huntly of my fainting spell. I am quite well again now."

They helped her into a seat, as though she were an invalid.

"I should send for the physician," the footman said, hovering beside her chair, eyes fixed worriedly upon her.

"No, you should not," she told him. "I had no dinner last night, which is the only reason for the dizzy spell, which has now passed. Thank you for your assistance, but you may now safely leave me."

Frowning, he did so.

"Did you receive a letter ordering you to give evidence at Viscount Inderly's trial too?"

He looked as if he wanted to say more about the other subject, but after a moment's hesitation, said that he had. With an effort, she responded, "It is a good thing. I am sure Aileas's parents will be glad to see this settled, so they can begin to move on." She hoped the trial would bring the justice they deserved for their daughter. Changing the subject, she said, "Please tell me about Miss Smith. Is she still a suspect?"

"No. She felt he had treated her generously. I do not believe there was any love on either side in that arrangement, so she had no reason to want him dead."

"Then, unless we are missing something, that just leaves Mrs Ainsley."

"I think..."

She was never to know what Mr MacPherson thought as Harriette swept into the room at that moment, her husband and Calum, the footman, behind her. "Lord Huntly was just informed that you fainted!"

Ishbel realised she had only told the footman not to speak to Harriette of what had happened, so he had gone straight to his master instead. She gave him a disappointed look. "I am perfectly well now."

"You said that at breakfast and it was clearly not true," Harriette said. "You must lie down immediately and Lord Huntly will send for the family physician."

"No," she said. "That is not necessary in the least. Harriette, might I speak to you alone please?"

Her cousin took a careful look at her, then ordered everyone else out. Mr MacPherson, following Lord Huntly's retreating figure, promised to call back this afternoon.

Ishbel waited until they were gone and then took a deep breath and told Harriette all that had happened yesterday. She was quite prepared to face censure for her own careless behaviour, but her cousin's wrath was aimed elsewhere. "When I have finished talking to Lord Moray," she promised, eyes flashing, "he will make sure all his acquaintances know that he was wrong to refer to you in such a way and that none of them will ever go near you from this time onwards. He will do so because, otherwise, he will never be accepted in Edinburgh society again."

Ishbel was not sure how Harriette could achieve such a result, but she did not doubt her. It was almost enough to make her feel sorry for Lord Moray and Hannam.

Finally able to shake free of her horror over the attack, she smiled.

29. ISHBEL FACES THE TON

ISHBEL'S INITIAL reaction was a fervent, "No!"

"You have to get back into society," Harriette said to her with uncharacteristic patience, "and it is better that you do so as quickly as possible, or you will fear it all the more."

Ishbel thought of all the insults and snubs that would be thrown at her then, far worse, she imagined being in a room filled with men like Lord Moray's friend. "I cannot."

"You are going," Harriette snapped and walked out of the room. Apparently her shows of patience were of short duration.

Ishbel glared after her departing figure. She had been through an ordeal and if she wanted to take some time off from mixing with Edinburgh's ton, then she would. She appealed later that day to Mr MacPherson for his support in this.

"I agree with Lady Huntly," he said. "You already have no liking for attending society events and, if you do not go back quickly, you will grow too nervous to ever do so. Besides, we have found out half the information needed to solve crimes at such entertainments. Do you really want to leave me to handle them alone?"

"No," she conceded.

"I will gladly attend the ball tonight, so you will not once be alone."

This instantly eased her nerves and she subdued her doubts and forced a smile to her face. "Very well. We will cope with it together."

She attended a couple of university lectures, one of which involved watching the dissection of a cadaver, where she felt a disturbing kinship with the dead person being cut apart. Her wounds from tonight would only be emotional ones, she told herself, and she cared nothing for such people's opinions anyway... but please let them not humiliate her in front of Ewan.

It was in this mood that she got dressed for the ball in a dark blue silk gown with pale blue lace-trimmed petticoats. Out of nowhere, when she was looking dispiritedly at her reflection in an ornate mirror, she thought of Miss McNeil, alone in that hideous gaol room with the knowledge that she could soon be hanged. This was nothing compared to what she was enduring and Ishbel was ashamed of herself for making so much of it. Of course she could do this.

"Thank you, Lucy," she said to her maid and turned and walked into the hallway and down the sweeping staircase.

Lord Huntly was standing waiting, looking wistfully in the direction of the library, while Harriette put on her gloves. "That dress is quite becoming," her cousin said, in an obvious effort to be encouraging.

"Yours is lovely." Even with her face painted fashionably but unflatteringly white, the amethyst-coloured dress suited Harriette perfectly.

"Yes, of course," her cousin agreed, as if this was an obvious fact.

The short carriage ride felt as if it took hours and she had to keep reminding herself to breathe. The ball was being held in the New Town Assembly Rooms and the whole of Edinburgh seemed to be in the enormous ballroom when they walked inside, the temperature stifling and the lights blinding after coming from the darkness and freezing cold outside.

A friend of Harriette's – a duchess of around fifty in a green gown and diamond jewellery – approached her at once, with the observation, "I knew we should not have accepted this invitation. Mrs McEllis has shown no discrimination at all in whom she has invited."

"How tedious," Harriette said. "Do you know Miss Campbell, my cousin?"

The duchess had never bothered to speak to Ishbel before and regarded her doubtfully through an eyeglass, before saying, "What a lovely child. It must be pleasant to belong to such an attractive family. I wish my son had considered such things when he chose his wife but no, he had to marry the Sinmore chit."

Ishbel wondered, with slight amusement, if the duchess's daughter-in-law viewed her in an equally unfavourable light.

"Miss Campbell."

She turned and, out of habit, curtsied, but went cold as she looked into the unpleasantly familiar features of Lord Moray. Why would he approach her like this? She glanced round, but Harriette seemed to be lost in conversation with her friend and Lord Huntly had left to fetch them refreshments.

Lord Moray seemed to have trouble meeting her eyes as he said, "Miss Campbell, would you allow me to offer my deepest apologies for any misunderstanding of my words that led to Mr Hannam's disgraceful manners towards you. His behaviour was unpardonable. His parents have removed him from Edinburgh to the country."

Ishbel wondered, with admiration, how Harriette had achieved this. "I accept your apology, sir, but our acquaintanceship is at an end."

"As you wish." He walked stiffly away just as Lord Huntly returned, handing Ishbel and Harriette a glass of ratafia. She thanked him and sipped her drink, feeling slightly more confident about being here, as she looked about for Mr MacPherson.

She caught sight of Mr Chiverton on the other side of the room conversing with a dozen or more people and, assuming Mr MacPherson was with the group, began to walk towards him. She paused at the sight of Lady Sarah Halsted nearby, talking with a short brunette lady, but she was no longer a suspect, so any further secrets she had were her own matter.

"...Scandalous!"

Ishbel looked sharply behind her and caught several women having a whispered conversation behind their fans. One of them looked directly at Ishbel and then hastily looked away.

"Miss Campbell." It was Lady Sarah's voice this time.

Ishbel turned to face the woman.

"I am astonished that you have the affrontery to appear here with decent people," Lady Sarah sneered in a voice loud enough to be overheard by a good many people. "Do you deny that you attempted to bribe my maid to tell you about me?"

Abruptly, Ishbel found that she was angry rather than embarrassed. She had put up with too much from people who had no right to judge her. "It is true," she said, meeting the lady's gaze.

"We thought you might be involved in your father's death and could not have been more wrong. We know you did not leave your father's house that night for some nefarious purpose."

She saw the realisation in the woman's eyes of where she had spent that night and the fact that Ishbel clearly knew about it.

"I am sure, however," Ishbel went on, "that you want your father's murder solved more than anyone and ask you to forgive me and my partner for acting inappropriately."

"I..." Lady Sarah glanced over at Lord Moray – who nodded and then looked quickly away – then back at Ishbel. "Yes, I, er, I do forgive you."

"That is kind of you. I am sure the mercy you have shown tonight will be returned to you one day." Ishbel saw the look of chagrined relief on her face, then turned away and walked through the puzzled onlookers to her cousin's side.

"How did you get her to publicly change her opinion?" Harriette asked in an undertone.

Ishbel smiled and whispered, "Blackmail."

"Well done!"

Mr MacPherson hurried to her side, appearance changed by his white wig, and she assumed he had seen what had been said to her and was concerned. Instead he said, "Miss Campbell, I have been looking for you. Mrs Ainsley has just arrived."

"Excuse me, please," she said to Harriette and her acquaintants. "We have a murder to solve."

Behind her, someone said, "What an odd young lady."

"That is my cousin," Harriette replied, pride in her voice.

"Forgive me for missing your arrival," Mr MacPherson said, as they walked.

"There is no need. I am quite well. In fact, I am beginning to enjoy the evening." She smiled to prove to him that she was sincere and he returned the smile, his handsome face brightening.

"There!" he said, nodding in the direction of a few people. "That is she."

Ishbel followed his gaze and saw the woman they had been looking for. Mrs Ainsley was a tall, willowy lady of around thirty with dark hair and a haughty expression. Ironically, Ishbel could see a resemblance between her and Mrs McNeil, although the latter had had a far more gracious countenance, even in gaol.

Mr MacPherson reached out to take Ishbel's arm, then hesitated, and she recalled her reaction the last time he had touched her. She deliberately placed her hand on the warm red silk of his arm, the touch making her hand tingle in a not unpleasant way. They exchanged glances and then approached the lady they suspected of murder.

30. EWAN'S HOPES

"I DINNA mind at all," Rabbie said, when Ewan suggested that he speak to Mrs Ainsley's servants. "I think I'm getting quite good at this."

"Your help has been invaluable," Ewan said as he buttoned up his striped waistcoat. "I truly hope she is our killer or that she at least hired someone to kill the duke."

"What if she dinna?"

"Then I can think of no one left but Miss McNeil and I do not want to believe her capable of such a crime. I liked her."

"Then you should trust that instinct. What did you think of Mrs Ainsley?"

Ewan and Miss Campbell had managed to get an introduction to her from a slight acquaintance of his last night. They had talked mostly of music but had also expressed their shock over the manner of the Duke of Raden's death. She had looked troubled, but she had spoken very little on the subject. "I formed no proper opinion. She kept her feelings hidden and her conversation light."

"That's not surprising, though, is it, sir?" Rabbie said, expertly tying Ewan's neckcloth. "She could hardly say that she'd been expecting a proposal from him any day and been driven to a murderous rage when he took up with an actress instead."

Ewan laughed. "It would have been helpful if she had said that, but, no, it was unlikely. Had she shown a marked liking for any other man at the ball, it would have suggested that she lost interest in the duke when he stopped seeing her. The fact she treated every man with polite indifference might be one small sign of her guilt." He put on a long redingote and paused to let Rabbie pull it slightly to the left over one shoulder, then straighten his neckcloth again, a frown of concentration on his face.

Rabbie stood back to check over his work and then gave a nod of satisfaction, communicating the fact that Ewan's appearance was acceptable. "Hopefully her staff will have some interesting things to tell me tonight and you can get the actress out of gaol. From the state your clothes were in when you visited that place, I wouldna want to see anyone I know locked up there."

"Nor I," Ewan agreed, hoping the bribe he had given to the guard would at least make the conditions bearable for Miss McNeil. He opened his money pouch and gave two shiny guineas to Rabbie. "This is for you to buy drinks for the servants tonight."

"That's far too much."

"Then buy something for yourself too. You have earned it with all the extra work you have done for me lately."

"Spending time at taverns isna much like work." He pocketed the money. "Thank you, sir. This will give my family a very cheerful Christmastide."

"I suppose it is not too long now."

"Just over a month."

And less than three weeks until Miss McNeil's trial began. This time last year he had been at his estate – he had been neglecting his responsibilities there recently but could not imagine leaving Miss Campbell for months. Perhaps, if he put a party together for the trip, she and her family would accompany him there.

"Are you all right, sir?"

He blinked and looked at Rabbie. "Wool-gathering, I fear. I think I will walk to my wigmaker's shop as the fresh air might have a positive effect on my mind."

Rabbie peered out of the bedroom window. "Well, it's no raining at least."

"Quite."

Ewan was less confident in his decision when he stepped outside and an icy blast of wind nearly knocked him over and made him shiver. It was only a short walk, he told himself, and he set forth at a swift pace.

His brain returned to the subject of Miss Campbell, as it so often did these days. She had seemed recovered from her recent mistreatment by the end of the ball. He understood how much strength of will she had needed to face another society gathering and was proud to love someone so brave. He had hoped that taking this case would help him understand why she felt unable to marry him, but he was as much in the dark as he had been when she turned down his proposal. He was sure she was fond of him and she had, after all, said that she could imagine marrying no one else.

He felt sure her present independence played some part in the decision. He should find some way to let her know he would never dream of asking her to change her life for him if they married, but he could not do so without repeating his proposal, and he did not want to do that while there was a strong chance she would reject him a second time.

Another gale made him stagger back a couple of steps and the forbidding weather seemed like a metaphor for the lack of progress in every part of his life at present. In answer to that, he lifted a booted foot and pushed forwards.

After a successful meeting with his wigmaker, he ran into McDonald, who had been visiting his tailor. They exchanged greetings and strolled together along the High Street.

"Chiverton says Alex is worried that the stress of this whole murder business is affecting Joe Fillinister," McDonald said. "Apparently Fillinister is being shouted at by their manager or director for not doing a good job rehearsing some play."

"It is hardly surprising. Miss McNeil is in an appalling place and our chance to help her is rapidly vanishing."

"I suppose they think of themselves as a family. The actors, that is. A lot of them do not seem to have anyone else."

"It must be a strange life." They paused in front of a barber's shop. "I fear I am beginning to doubt Miss McNeil's innocence. It seems unlikely that a widow would murder the Duke of Raden simply for not proposing to her."

"Women take these subjects to heart. Their reputations are affected."

That was true enough, although it was not just women. He had been strongly affected by Miss Campbell's rejection.

As if he had said this aloud, McDonald said, "I would have expected you to have asked Miss Campbell to marry you by now. I hope my doubts on the matter did not put you off."

Ewan smiled at him. "They did not. I made the offer..."

"Oh!" McDonald pulled a face. "Forgive my blunder. I had begun to think the two of you very well suited."

"I am not giving up," Ewan said. "Not at all."

31. A ROUGH-LOOKING MAN

IT WAS another day until Ishbel saw Mr MacPherson again. She had been attending lectures all day yesterday, but today she had an appointment with him to hear what his valet had managed to find out about Mrs Ainsley and later he would be attending the formal dinner party Harriette was hosting.

He was announced shortly after breakfast and they exchanged bow and curtsy and then smiled in greeting. He was looking particularly handsome in a velvet waistcoat and breeches, the shade of which brought out the vibrant green of his eyes.

"We should retreat to the library," she told him, leading the way. "Harriette is shouting at all the servants for not setting up everything the way she wishes for her dinner party."

"How unpleasant for them."

"Indeed and it is likely that she will find a reason to shout at us if she sees us."

"Then we should certainly stay out of sight," he said cheerfully, as they sat down near to the marble fireplace. "Rabbie spoke to a couple of Mrs Ainsley's servants, who said she had been increasingly irritable in recent months due – they assumed – to the Duke of Raden's absence. He had been attentive to her for more than a six-month then, with everyone waiting for news of their engagement, stopped calling to see her. The servants did not think she knew about Mrs McNeil as when she was told about his death, and where he was found, they saw her reaction and she seemed appalled, caught between grief and fury."

"Then she did not kill him," Ishbel concluded, disappointed.

"I am not so certain. Someone described as a rough-looking man visited her home about a week before the duke's death and she spoke to him privately."

"But why would she have wanted him dead if she did not know she had been replaced in his affections?"

"I cannot answer that, but perhaps the man she spoke to can. I have asked the caddie, Jed, to try to find him. The man had a distinctive scar – a burn mark – on the back of his hand, so it should hopefully be possible to trace him."

"I hope he will be willing to talk."

"If he is a criminal then the offer of payment from us should loosen his tongue."

"Good."

Their conversation was interrupted when Harriette strode into the room and said in an accusing tone, "Have either of you seen the oriental vase that was in the dining room?"

"Did you not have it moved upstairs last year when you put Lord Huntly's gift of the porcelain figurines in its place?" Ishbel asked.

"Yes." Harriette had clearly forgotten this, but she covered the fact with a confident manner. "That is correct." She marched out again, a footman trailing behind her.

"I hope, for everyone's sake, that this dinner party goes smoothly," Ishbel said.

"Are you nervous about it?"

"No, surprisingly I am not. Perhaps I have moved past the point where I care what most of them think. So many people have secrets, whether innocent or dangerous ones, that I begin to think I cannot possibly be any worse a person than them."

She saw his startled reaction to these words. "Why should you possibly imagine that you ever had any cause to be compared unfavourably with...?"

Harriette walked back in again and sighed heavily. "Are the two of you still here? I have work to do!"

"Perhaps I can assist you." Ishbel got to her feet and Mr MacPherson did the same.

"Oh, very well," she agreed grudgingly, then gestured towards Mr MacPherson with her fan, "but you can leave here and not return until tonight. You are of no use at all."

He threw Ishbel a bright-eyed look of amusement and bowed to the women. "Then I will see you again this evening."

"What are you smiling about?" Harriette demanded of Ishbel.

"I am looking forward to your dinner party."

"Hmm."

Ishbel was happy to greet Ewan as one of the first guests that evening. She was so lost in conversation with him that it took her a while to notice that the room was considerably less full than usual. Harriette's events were normally exclusive and highly sought after. Surely her presence here was not ruining the situation for her cousin again? She looked more carefully around the drawing room and caught a number of glances in her direction from people engaged in hushed conversations. Worse, when one lady caught her eye, she frowned and looked away in a deliberate snub. The reactions themselves bothered her little but she hated to think that in her determination to make her own decisions about her life, Harriette was the one who would suffer.

"Monsieur MacPherson!"

Ishbel turned and saw the young French lady who had insisted upon dancing with Mr MacPherson at the ball last week and had shown such a liking for him. What was she doing here?

He bowed to her. "It is a pleasure to see you again, Mademoiselle Moreau. Is the Comtesse Moreau with you?"

"She is convas-conversing with Madame Linbarr."

"And have you been introduced to Miss Campbell?"

The two of them curtsied to each other and Ishbel thought she saw an assessing look on the younger woman's face, but it was gone before she could be sure.

"Miss Campbell is cousin to Lady Huntly, your hostess. She lives here."

"How charming for you," Mademoiselle Moreau said, smiling at Ishbel and looking utterly innocent. Perhaps she was simply trying to fit in here and in her new country. "This is such a beau – a lovely house and very elegant."

"Thank you. I believe my cousin made a lot of changes when she married Lord Huntly, to make it more fashionable."

"And your gown is very pretty."

"That is kind. Yours is too."

"It is new," she said, turning to include Mr MacPherson in her smile.

"It is lovely," he told her politely, with an awkward side glance at Ishbel.

A gentleman every bit as young as the Mademoiselle appeared with a glass of lemonade for her and she thanked him with a smile, before expertly ignoring him.

"Is there to be dancing soon?" she asked Mr MacPherson. "You know how much I enjoy to dance."

"No, not tonight."

"Then you will dance with me on another occasion?"

The lady was determined and Ishbel could not fault her taste, but her flirtatious attitude towards Mr MacPherson was highly irritating. Ishbel tried to engage the lady's admirer in conversation, but he spoke awkwardly to her and kept stealing glances at Mademoiselle Moreau. When the butler announced dinner, she could not have been more relieved. Mr MacPherson came before her in precedence for the procession into the dining room and had to escort an older titled lady, but as long as it was not Mademoiselle Moreau, Ishbel did not care who he spent the time with.

In the dining room she looked for the first time at the names on the table that told everyone where to sit. She hoped she was near to Mr MacPherson or, at the very least, that he was as far away from the Mademoiselle as possible.

Harriette nudged her arm and gestured with her fan to a seat close to her own and Ishbel, seeing Mr MacPherson's name written on the place beside hers, smiled her thanks to Harriette and sat down. She watched happily as the Mademoiselle and her mother took seats further down the table, on the opposite side, almost invisible behind a large sugar sculpture.

Her smile faded as Lady Tinbough took a seat almost directly opposite. She had seen the woman a few times here and at other functions and Lady Tinbough had been polite and given no sign that she blamed Ishbel and Mr MacPherson for the imprisonment of her son. Nonetheless, Ishbel felt uncomfortable over it and disliked the thought of the pain she had brought to Lady Tinbough's life, who had done nothing to cause blame or censure.

Out of politeness, she looked to the gentleman seated on the opposite side of her, whose wife was friends with Harriette. "How are you and Mrs Kinson enjoying the season?"

"We have done nothing to get us arrested, Miss Campbell," he said shortly, "so I doubt you care."

The woman beside him giggled and there was a lull in several conversations while various sets of eyes swivelled in the direction of Mr MacPherson and her. Against her will, she felt a blush stain her cheeks. She glanced round and received a number of hostile looks.

"This meal is wonderful," Mr MacPherson said hastily to her. "Your family's chef is a true expert."

"Yes," she agreed, looking blankly at the plate in front of her. "My cousin could not have found anyone better. We are fortunate."

"I normally prefer summer food as I enjoy the wider range of fruit and vegetables available..."

They managed to sustain this conversation until everyone within hearing distance of them was sufficiently bored as to return to their own discussions.

The evening passed slowly.

32. THE NATURE OF LOVE

"I AM sorry that your dinner party was less successful than usual because of me," Ishbel said when the last of the guests had left and the servants were cleaning and tidying around them as they sat in the parlour.

"It was only one evening," Harriette said. "They will have something other than you to chatter and complain about by tomorrow."

Ishbel would not be put off. "I thought only of my own wishes in pursuing the solving of crimes and did not consider how much it would affect you and Lord Huntly. It would make your lives easier were I to leave here..."

Harriette made a sharp, dismissing gesture. "We have discussed this matter and this is your home. You place far too much importance on one event."

"If Mr MacPherson and I continue our investigations, people will continue to snub us. It will not just be one event."

"Then our family will have a little notoriety. So be it." She dismissed further protests with a look. "The subject is closed."

Ishbel nodded, relieved she would not have to proceed with her offer to live elsewhere. "Why did you invite the Comtesse and her daughter tonight?"

"Forgive me," Harriette said dryly. "I was not aware that they were enemies of yours."

"No, of course they are not!"

"They are friends of a friend. Well, an acquaintance. Someone I generally do not dislike. Anyway, you will find yourself far less prone to these moments of jealousy when you and Mr MacPherson are married. I am surprised it has taken him this long to propose to you." She saw Ishbel's expression and her eyes widened. "When did he propose to you?"

"After the emerald necklace matter."

Harriette was silent for time. "What will you say when he asks you again?"

"He will not," Ishbel insisted, although her heart jumped a bit at the thought. "We are friends now and work partners."

"You are far more than friends. He supports all your bizarre ideas and your desires for your life, even the patently stupid ones. That is what a husband does; a good one, anyway."

Ishbel thought about Lord Huntly and then she thought about her deceased family. "My parents had a terrible marriage."

"Many people do," Harriette said dismissively. "What does that have to do with you?"

"My mother felt trapped. My father was angry all the time. I never want my life to be like that."

"Why should it? Is Mr MacPherson anything like either of your parents? Has he ever shown anything other than affection and loyalty to you?"

"No," she admitted, realising as she said it that it was the truth. He was everything and more that she could possibly want. And she loved him. She had loved him for months, but she had refused to admit it to herself. "I was not close to either of my parents," she said with difficulty. "I am not certain that either of them loved me. What if there was a reason for that, something unlovable inside me?"

"I cannot speak for your father, but your mother was even worse at expressing affection than I am. I do not doubt that she loved you, however she may have behaved, and I know there is nothing wrong with you because you are my family and I love you."

Ishbel swallowed down a lump in her throat and reached out an arm, only to be waved away.

"I avoid embracing people wherever possible," Harriette said curtly, then she added, "I hope you realise that it would be extremely foolish to turn down the marriage proposal of the man you love more than once."

Ishbel thought she might be right.

33. VIOLENCE

ISHBEL RECEIVED the news that Mr MacPherson and Jed Cassell were here to see her the next day with pleasure. The inquiry into the murder had come to a standstill and she was eager to move forward with it again.

She had a footman bring them into the library and then, having admitted her feelings about Mr MacPherson to herself last night, did not know quite how to behave with him. Mr Cassell was still wearing his blue caddie's apron but he had taken off his cap and clutched it in his hands, once again showing discomfort at being in such a large expensively furnished house.

She greeted him warmly to allay his unease and said, "Did you manage to find anything out about Mrs Ainsley's visitor?"

"Aye, miss. It was a criminal called John Marne, but I'm afraid I dinna think it was anything to do with the Duke of Raden. Marne's been asking around about items stolen in a robbery from Mrs Ainsley's house, so it looks as if she hired him to get back something of value to her."

Ishbel glanced at Mr MacPherson, who gave a shrug and said, "It seems as if she was never a suspect after all. Nothing Rabbie or Jed here has found out suggests she was involved."

"No." Ishbel did not want to believe that, when Mrs Ainsley was the only person other than Miss McNeil who had a motive for the crime. "Just because she has him looking into the robbery, does not mean she did not also hire him for another purpose. Mr Cassell, is Mr Marne the kind of man who might commit a murder?"

"He's a dangerous thug, Miss Campbell. You dinna want to go anywhere near him."

She turned back to Mr MacPherson. "Mrs Ainsley could have got him to kill the duke."

He thought about it, then said to the caddie, "Is there anyone we could speak to who might know more about his criminal activities?"

Mr Cassell gave this some thought. "He mixes with a lot of bad people and commits crimes alongside some of them. There is one person, though: Micky Loughlin. He's mates with Marne's brother, but he hates Marne. He might be willing to answer your questions for a fee and he'll be working at the Leith docks for the rest of the day."

"Then we should go and speak to him," Ishbel said to Mr MacPherson, who agreed at once. "Mr Cassell, would you be willing to accompany us and point him out?"

"Of course, miss."

She collected her hat, gloves and mantelet and they headed out into the cold, clinging fog to Mr MacPherson's carriage. The weather grew even more icy as they got closer to the sea, although the surrounding landscape was attractive to look out at, the mist giving the estuary, woodland and pastures an aura of mystery.

They descended from the carriage at the docks area, which was full of working-class men, loud noise and the odours of fish and brine. It took them a bit of time to find Mr Loughlin, a strong-looking man of around thirty with a weathered face. He viewed them with suspicion when Mr Cassell introduced them, even when Mr MacPherson offered him some coins from his money pouch.

"What's that for then?" he asked, not taking the money.

"We simply want to ask you a few questions about John Marne," Mr MacPherson said. "We are looking into a criminal matter and need to find out what Marne's connection is to Mrs Ainsley."

He looked doubtfully at them and then his eyes came to rest on the offered coins. "She was robbed and asked him to find the thief and get back some family heirloom for her."

"Was there nothing else she needed his help with?" Ishbel asked.

"No, miss. He's been bragging about the money he made from that lady, because he'd already known who'd done the robbery. He got the painting back, paid off the thief and he said Mrs Ainsley was happy; said it was even easier money than robbing someone."

Mr MacPherson gave him the money and they began to walk back to the carriage.

"I am sorry," Ishbel said to him. "You were right – Mrs Ainsley was never a very likely suspect and, with no other connection to anyone criminal, she obviously had nothing to do with the murder."

"It was worth..." Mr MacPherson broke off as a shout sounded from behind them. They turned around to see a large unkempt-looking man striding towards them.

"That's John Marne's brother," Mr Cassell said. "Perhaps you'd better leave me to sort this out with him."

"That might put you in danger," Ishbel objected. "I am sure we can explain to him that the topic is resolved."

The man caught up with them and took a long, frowning look at each of them. He smelt of sweat and fish and there was a hard look in his eyes. "What are the three of you asking questions about my brother for? What d'you want with him?"

"Nothing," Mr MacPherson said, raising his hands in a placating gesture. "We had some questions about a crime, but..."

"Ewan!" Ishbel said urgently, as she saw that two more men had got behind them, blocking the way back to their carriage.

"There is nothing for us to quarrel about," Mr MacPherson told Marne, "so I suggest you ask your friends to leave us to discuss this calmly."

"You're trying to cause trouble for John."

"No. We..."

One moment they were talking and the next, one of the other men had taken a punch at Mr Cassell. Mr MacPherson tried to intervene, but Marne grabbed his arm and then all three dock men were attacking her friends. Ishbel looked in one direction then another for someone who could help them, but the other workers were ignoring the fight and remaining a good distance from them.

Marne punched Mr MacPherson in the face, knocking him down. Ishbel shrieked and ran forward, into the middle of the chaos. She had to do something to stop this. She never should have suggested that they visit this place. Mr MacPherson pulled himself unsteadily to his feet and put a hand on her arm, trying to get her behind him for protection, but she refused to move.

"Listen to me!" she shouted at Marne and there must have been some authority in her tone, as he looked around. "Please listen. This is a mistake. We thought your brother might be involved in a murder, but I promise you that we were wrong. It was the matter he was hired for by Mrs Ainsley..."

"... There was nothing illegal in that!" Marne said.

"We know," she agreed, silently begging him to listen to her. He must, or her companions might not survive this encounter. "We were wrong. If you let us leave now we will not have you charged for attacking us and you will never see us again."

Marne looked steadily at her for a long moment, his expression unreadable. Ishbel pushed down rising panic and forced herself to stand still and upright. She continued to meet the hard gaze of the man she was certain was capable of a lot worse than this. Finally, Marne yelled at his friends to back off and, when they stopped fighting, Ishbel was able to start breathing again.

Mr Cassell had blood running down from his nose and Mr MacPherson's eye was swelling. She needed to get them safely away.

Marne was not finished. "Do you promise that that's really all this is about? You'll not try to pin the blame on John for anything else?"

"You have my word," Ishbel said and Mr MacPherson reiterated her promise.

Marne jerked his head at his two friends and they slowly moved, expressions wild as if they were reluctant to give up the fight. They swaggered past Ishbel's group and stood, in a threatening manner, behind Marne.

"Don't come here again," he said.

34. A TROUBLING CONCLUSION

"THIS WAS all my doing," Miss Campbell said, complexion so white that Ewan feared she might faint. "I am so sorry. If only I had accepted that Mrs Ainsley was innocent when Mr Cassell explained about the robbery."

"We did not know for certain at that point," Ewan said. "Speaking to the brother seemed to be a reasonable way of settling whether or not John Marne was involved in the murder."

They were at Ewan's house where Rabbie was tending to his eye and his butler was cleaning the blood from Jed's face. Miss Campbell sat close by, watching the proceedings with a haunted expression and clutching her reticule with hands that five minutes earlier had been shaking. Luckily, their injuries were not bad. If not for Miss Campbell's intervention, the situation could have become far worse.

"I shouldna have suggested talking to Micky Loughlin," Jed responded, as he sat on a dining chair and gingerly touched his nose. "I knew he'd tell Paul Marne about it, but I never thought Marne would dare to attack two important people like you."

"No one is to blame," Ewan told him, "and it is all over now. It is simply a lesson that we need to be more diplomatic in our questioning of people in future. Jed's nose is not broken, is it, MacCuaig?"

"No, sir," the butler answered a touch dismissively, "and it's stopped bleeding now, so he'll be fine."

Ewan paid Jed a generous sum for his help and for the trouble they had caused him, then sent him home in the carriage to change, since his clothes had got an unpleasant mixture of blood, mud and refuse on them. As he observed this, he realised his own outfit was no better; no wonder Rabbie had such an unhappy expression.

"I should put on fresh clothes," he told Miss Campbell, "and, for your reputation's sake, you must not remain any longer at my home. It is only a short journey so will a sedan chair be suitable to convey you to your house?"

"Yes, of course," she said. "Will you be fit to call on me later to discuss the case, or should you rest?"

"I am already recovered," he reassured her. "I will see you soon." He ordered MacCuaig to arrange for her transport and she stood up to leave, before hesitating and, instead of moving towards the door, she walked up to him. She touched her gloved hand to his cheek and he felt the light touch with an intensity that blotted out everything but her.

"Ewan..."

He stared at her as the atmosphere between them changed. She was so close and looking at him with an expression of concern and warmth. His desire to kiss her was almost overwhelming, but of course that was out of the question. It was enough for him to believe that she might want the same.

She let her hand fall away and said to Rabbie, who was looking fixedly at the floor, "Look after him."

The valet looked up, a sparkling expression in his eyes. "I will, Miss Campbell."

Her gaze met Ewan's once more and he could almost see his future with her in that look, before she turned and left.

"Is this business of looking into crimes really worth threats to your life?" Chiverton asked, observing Ewan's eye with a frown. He had called at the house just as Ewan was about to leave to visit Miss Campbell and, as eagerly as he wanted to see her again right away, he could not avoid Chiverton's stream of questions about the fight.

"It was never that," he said. "I could have got a worse blow in a friendly boxing match."

"And Miss Campbell was with you? She was not injured?"

"No, thankfully, although the incident shook her."

"I should think so," Chiverton agreed. "It has shaken me! You must be more careful in future, old fellow."

"I will. You have my word. Miss Campbell was in danger, which is unacceptable. We will be more cautious from now on. Indeed, I doubt there is much left for us to do, although I fear we are reaching a conclusion that will make Joe Fillinister very unhappy."

"You think Kenina actually killed the duke?"

"We have no one left to consider for the crime. We have thoroughly looked into both the duke's life and hers and I do not believe there is anything new for us to uncover."

"Poor Joe and, even if she did kill him, poor Kenina. She will hang. It is a horrific punishment for her to endure."

Chiverton left shortly after this and Ewan took his carriage, now returned from taking Jed home, to Miss Campbell's house, the tall pale building as familiar as his own these days. Miss Campbell was writing pages of notes in the library, several medical texts open in front of her, but she stoppered the ink bottle and put down her quill as soon as he arrived and stood to curtsy and take a closer look at his eye. It felt rather tender and swollen but otherwise not bad, however judging from Miss Campbell's wince, it had gained some brighter colours than usual.

"The swelling will have vanished by tomorrow," he said before she could take the blame for what had happened again, "and it will be back to normal in a few more days."

"We should never have gone to the docks." She sat down in a different seat than the one she had previously used, closer to the fire, and he took the chair just a couple of feet away, facing her.

"We are still learning how to conduct investigations and if we have learnt a lesson today in proceeding in a more careful way, then that is to the good. Have you considered what our next step should be?"

"I can think of little more that we can do," she admitted with regret. "Miss McNeil appears to be our only remaining suspect."

"I agree."

She paused, looking into the flames, face and hair bathed in a warm glow that made him unable to look away. "We must speak to Miss McNeil again."

"Yes," he agreed. "While we seem to have run out of other options, I still cannot picture her committing the murder. We have to be sure of her guilt before we finish our involvement and let her go to trial."

She got to her feet. "Then let us go now and see what she says."

35. A DIFFERENT SIDE OF THE STORY

THE OLD Tolbooth gaol was every bit as horrific as Ishbel had remembered, from the stench of human waste and unwashed bodies to the callous treatment of its inmates. Miss McNeil, at least, looked more alert than when they had seen her last, her room cleaner, and she thanked them both profusely for gaining this better treatment from the guards. Her pleasure at seeing them made Ishbel feel even worse about their purpose here.

"Have you discovered who killed the Duke of Raden?" she asked eagerly.

"I fear we have ruled out every possible suspect," Ewan said and they saw the light fade from her eyes.

"Then I will hang for an ugly crime that I did not commit."

Ishbel walked up to her, taking her hand. "You have nothing to lose now. Is there anything at all you have not told us? Anything you have not been entirely honest about?"

Miss McNeil sighed and gave a short nod. "I painted a picture of my life that was lovelier than the reality. I was lying to myself more than you. Richard – the Duke of Raden – did love me; I am certain of that. However... I believed too much in his romantic words. I told you I didn't want him to marry me, but that wasn't true. Recently something happened..." She broke off and Ishbel could see indecision in her blue eyes before she continued. "A week before Richard was killed, I believed I might be with child. I told him about it, with the wild idea he might suggest marriage, but he was furious, saying the scandal would destroy him. From what he said it was clear he'd end all contact with me rather than face the mockery and dislike of his peers. We argued. I was miserable for several days and, of course, I discovered at that time that I was not going to have a baby after all. My belief that he still loved me was destroyed and I considered never seeing him again. I felt he deserved to know that there wouldn't be a child and sent him a note, and he immediately came to see me, with a long stream of apologies and an expensive gift of jewellery. I was confused about my own feelings and let him convince me we should continue as before. However, I don't know if I could've stayed with him much longer. He died the night after his apology. I'm sorry I lied to you. It was too humiliating for me to think about."

Ishbel tried to take in this new information, shocked to discover this ugly side to the duke nearly everyone had adored. If the discovery was unpleasant for her, it must have been unbearable for Miss McNeil. She looked the other woman in the eyes. "Did you kill him in anger for how he had treated you?"

"No. I know you have little reason to believe me now, but I truly didn't kill him."

Ishbel was not sure whether she believed the words or not.

"Who knew about this?" Mr MacPherson asked.

"No one."

"Are you certain?" he checked.

She bit her lip, brow furrowed. "Well, I suppose one of the staff in my household might have overheard the argument, but that would be no reason for any of them to harm him. I..." She turned pale and Mr MacPherson caught her, putting an arm round her waist, before she could collapse. He carefully lowered her to the rough floorboards and she leaned forward, a hand over her face, as she breathed in and out. After a moment, eyes still closed, she said, "I'm sorry. It suddenly hit me that I'm really going to die."

"We should not wear you out further," Ishbel said, "but this might give us new suspects to consider. Do not give up hope entirely."

Miss McNeil opened her eyes and gave a wan smile. She looked very small, sitting hugging her knees on the floor. "You're both very kind. You've already done more than anyone could've asked for, when you owed me nothing. I'm really grateful."

She sounded as if she was saying goodbye to them.

36. REASSURANCE

AS THEY left the gaol, Ishbel thought about how it would feel for a woman to endure weeks of torment, knowing she could not prove her innocence and that she would hang for the crime of murder.

"... Lady Huntly's relation!"

Ishbel looked up, seeing two smartly dressed women on the street nearby. She recognised them both as wealthy married women who often attended balls and dinner parties, but she only knew the name of one of them.

"Disgusting," the unknown woman responded, pitching her words to be heard by Ishbel. "Her mother was no better than a harlot and she is just the same."

Ishbel gasped. She wanted to say something in defence of both Mama and herself, but she could not argue with a stranger in the middle of a public street. In any case, she was horrified to realise, she had no idea what she could say. She was here to visit a working-class woman who was accused of murdering her lover. No upper-class lady would see anything respectable in that.

Mr MacPherson held out his hand to help her into his carriage and, as she took it, she saw him aim a cold glare at the gossiping ladies. So he had heard more humiliating comments being made to her. She avoided his eyes as he took a seat opposite her in the carriage and the vehicle began to move.

"Pay them no attention," he said to her.

She looked out of the window, feeling the heat rising to her cheeks. "Of course not."

"Miss Campbell, I hope you would never believe for even a moment that such foolish comments could ever affect my liking and admiration for you."

She turned her head to face him. "I believe most people would say that I am no longer respectable."

"I think you exaggerate but, in any case, I solve mysteries alongside you. Do you really think I would be such a hypocrite as to think less of you for doing the same thing as me?" He looked appalled at the idea and she could not help but smile, heartened by his reaction.

"I would not expect that from you, although few other men would think it unfair to expect better behaviour from women than they themselves showed, just as few members of the ton will fail to judge you badly for associating with me."

"Ishbel," he said softly. "You have done nothing wrong and I esteem no one more highly than you. If everyone but you disowned me, I would remain content."

She had to blink away tears at these words, her embarrassment fading away. If he felt no cause to think less of her because of her mother's affairs and her own unconventional behaviour, then she had little to fear from life. It rendered the gossip about her meaningless.

"I want you to know that there is also no one's opinion that means more to me than yours." She wanted to say that she made up her mind years ago not to marry, having only had the example of a bad one and too naive to understand how different a good marriage could be. She wanted him to ask her to marry him, so she could give him a different answer, but the words would not come to her.

She was struggling to think of a way to speak of her feelings when he said, "I thought that seeing Miss McNeil might bring a feeling of closure to the case, but it had the opposite effect on me."

"Yes," she agreed, half thankful of the change of subject. This was much easier to discuss, although she was frustrated with herself for not being braver. "I think she is innocent, but how can we possibly prove it to a judge and jury in less than two weeks?"

"We must look deeper into both the duke and Miss McNeil's lives in search of someone new with a motive to kill him."

"Could her confession today lead us in a new direction?" she wondered. "Everyone thought the duke loved her and many thought that he might marry her. But she has no family and we have found no evidence of anyone being in love with her, so who could have been angered to the degree of committing murder because of the duke's treatment of her?"

"Joe Fillinister seems more fond of her than anyone else, but he did not know of the argument and, as you say, it would take a lot to make someone commit murder. I cannot imagine any of Miss McNeil's servants would feel so protective of her that they would kill for her, having only presumably known her since the duke bought her house and hired them, and they are the only ones who might have known about her falling out with the duke."

"Mr Fillinister knows the most about her life and friends so I think we should talk again to him," she suggested. "If he can suggest nothing better, then we can look into who might have found out about the argument between Miss McNeil and the duke."

"Good idea."

It was dark outside now and past the time when she should have begun changing her clothes for dinner. "Shall we visit him the day after tomorrow, after Viscount Inderly's trial?"

"Certainly. I will send him a letter, so that he expects us." They agreed on a time and he added, "I am not sure what to expect at the trial. Are you nervous?"

"A little." That was an understatement, but this was about Aileas's parents, not her. "I hope we may do some good there."

"Indeed." His tone was more cheerful as he said, "Are you still intending to attend the ball at the New Assembly Rooms tomorrow evening?"

She looked at him in confusion. "Was I ever meaning to go?"

He grimaced. "Lady Huntly led me to believe you would both be there."

Of course she had. Nevertheless, after Mr MacPherson's reassurance that unkind comments would not change his regard for her, she had no reason to fear the event and Harriette might not have been wrong when she said that Ishbel could only prove that she had nothing to be ashamed of by facing them all. "Does that mean you will be at the ball?" she checked.

"It does."

She resolutely dismissed from her mind the disastrous nature of recent entertainments and said, "I will be happy to see you there."

37. FADING HOPE

"LET ME see if I understand this correctly," Mr Braden, Viscount Inderly's solicitor, said to Ishbel, looking at her with cold eyes and a down-turned mouth. Behind him sat a roomful of people, not just Aileas's parents and friends, but many of Edinburgh's ton as well. "You, an unmarried lady, or a woman at least..." There was some laughter at this insult. "... spoke with criminals and vagabonds who told you that my client was guilty of some sort of crime?"

"I asked questions of..." Her words came out shaky and almost inaudible, so she swallowed, and began again. "I asked questions of a number of respectable people who identified Viscount Inderly as having bought a pendant for Aileas Jones..."

"Ah, yes, the pendant. That is why my client has been sitting in a gaol room!"

There was more laughter and Ishbel's glare fell onto the figure beside him of the viscount, who looked perfectly dressed and alert. Clearly he had not had to suffer the same discomforts as Miss McNeil during his weeks under arrest. She had already given her account of the crime in answer to the prosecution solicitor's questions and, by now, with this interrogation from a new source, the ordeal seemed never-ending.

"Your client confessed to having forced his attentions on Aileas Jones," she said loudly and the room fell silent, "and, having got her with child, he took her for an illegal operation with an unlicensed student of medicine. He told Mr MacPherson and me this."

"Lord Inderly denies any such speech and claims that you and your, er, *gentleman acquaintance*..." His emphasis put a sordid complexion on the last words. "... have some form of vendetta against him, perhaps because he comes from a decent background, whereas you do not. Do you have some grievance against him or against good society in general because of the shame your own mother brought to your family with her immoral relationships with a variety of men?"

Harriette was in the audience, having to hear this, along with dozens of others. Ishbel could not look at her and turned desperately at the judge. "Must I answer such a question?"

Belatedly, the prosecution solicitor stood up and said, "I object to this entire subject as an irrelevant one and a clear attempt to discredit my witness."

The judge was silent for a long moment, then, just as she was hoping he would take her side, said calmly, "If the witness has some reason for wanting to cause the viscount harm, then we need to hear of it."

Ishbel clenched her fists and said, "I never met Viscount Inderly before looking into this crime and I swear to this court that I have no personal reason for wanting to cause him harm. I was requested by the viscount's mother, Lady Tinbough, to begin looking into the matter..."

The defence solicitor spoke over her, asking in a fake shocked tone, "Lady Tinbough asked you to find out about the death of a maid?"

"No, she had lost an emerald necklace..."

She was once again interrupted. "So you found her necklace?"

"No. It..."

"So you were unable to solve the crime you were asked to look into but you expect the jury to believe that you were able to solve the death of Aileas Jones?"

"Viscount Inderly confessed!" she exclaimed.

"So you say," he responded dismissively, "but I am sure the jury will know whose word to trust. You are dismissed."

Her legs were shaking so much they would barely support her as she left the stand and walked out of the room. Now it was Ewan's turn and she would not even be allowed to hear the questions asked of him. She could only hope with everything in her that this ordeal would serve a worthwhile purpose and the viscount would be properly punished.

"We have ruled out everyone we suspected of the murder, so we need help from you in order to continue the investigation," Ewan said to Fillinister, as he and Miss Campbell sat in the parlour of his lodging house. The trial of Viscount Inderly the previous day had gone on well into the evening but, as witnesses, he and Miss Campbell had not been allowed to listen to the case. It was probably a good thing as Miss Campbell had clearly been shaken by what was said to her on the stand, although she would not tell him what that was. They were awaiting news of the verdict, something that kept distracting Ewan, but he forced himself to concentrate on the actor opposite him.

The fact that they had got nowhere with the investigation so far was clearly a blow to the man. "If there was anyone I suspected, I'd tell you at once, but there's no one. Surely a man as powerful as the duke had enemies?"

"Not really," Miss Campbell said. "He was generally well-liked. He had good manners and a good name, so the ton thought well of him and he seemed to treat others in a generous manner, so they had no reason to dislike him. The only person we could find who was angry with him was a friend who had an alibi for the night he died."

"We know there was another side to him, though," Ewan said. "He had an argument with Miss McNeil shortly before he died that proved he could behave in a callous way. Is there anyone who might have objected to that?"

"All of her friends including me would've been angry if the duke was cruel to Kenina, but a number of us feared the relationship wouldn't last. If it ended, we'd want to look after her, but some angry words wouldn't be reason to kill him."

"You are absolutely certain you know of no one who might have been in love with her?" he asked.

"As a good actress and attractive woman, she had her share of admirers, but none recently were persistent and she loved the duke, so she encouraged no one. I honestly can't think of anyone; I wish I could. But, if you can't prove someone else committed the crime, surely there's some way to prove Kenina didn't kill him?"

"I fear not," Miss Campbell said. "He was killed in her house and the servants were already asleep when he arrived. There is no one who saw what happened and the house was not broken into. He could have invited someone else inside but, unless we can prove that to be the case and name the person, then Miss McNeil remains, in the jury's eyes, the most likely suspect."

"Do you really think they could hang her with no proof that she harmed the duke?"

"As far as we can prove," Ewan said, "the night he died, there was no one in the house except for Miss McNeil and her servants. None of them had any grudge against the duke and Miss McNeil was the only person who fled from the scene."

"I agreed with her that she had to go," he said. "It's my fault. I knew they'd suspect her but, if I'd told her to stay..."

"... Then her trial would already be over," Ewan told him, "and, with no one else with entry to the house and a motive for the crime, she would already have been sentenced to hang. You have no reason to reproach yourself and we will keep working to find the real killer."

"Thank you, sir. I'm very grateful."

The words were similar to the ones Miss McNeil had used and Ewan feared that, like her, Fillinister was losing hope.

38. UNEXPECTED HELP

ISHBEL HAD been at the ball for less than five minutes when a well-respected matron turned her back as Ishbel approached the group, cutting her. She ignored the slight and the resulting giggles, an easy task when Mr MacPherson approached her with not just his friends, Mr Chiverton and Mr McDonald, but another man as well. The gentleman was introduced as Mr Liddon, who had had a novel published the previous year and was interested to hear how she and Mr MacPherson had begun solving crimes for a new novel he was planning.

By the time Ishbel had conversed with these companions, two hours had passed in an unexpectedly pleasant fashion and she accepted Mr MacPherson's request of a dance with hardly any misgivings. If she made a fool of herself by being clumsy, she thought, then it would be nothing she had not done before and it would be the least embarrassing thing to have recently happened to her in public.

"What have you told people about your eye?" she asked him as she took his hand and walked into the middle of the ballroom with the other dancers. His eye still looked painfully bruised and sore from the punch he had taken, but he always said it was nothing. He was a brave man.

"I told my friends the truth and accepted a fair rebuke from Chiverton about being more careful and advice from McDonald about how to fight. I misled anyone else who asked with the tale of an accidental knock received during a friendly boxing match."

"How dangerous such sports are," she said in a mocking manner.

"Indeed. I recall a duel that nearly finished me."

She smiled as she recalled that no actual duelling had occurred on that occasion. The dance began and she wondered if her fear over losing him in that duel was what had caused her to fall in love with him. She thought it had probably begun before then, but she was not certain. Perhaps the first embers had come to life when she met him in the courtroom of William Brodie's trial: a stranger with striking eyes and a kind voice.

She watched him as they moved through the steps of the dance and, equally often, found his eyes upon her face. Despite everything, he still loved her. She thought now of the life they could have together and there was nothing in it that worried or scared her. They could be happy. She just had to find a way to let him know that her feelings had changed and why.

His hand was entwined with hers again as the dance ended.

"How prettily the two of you dance together," a plump lady of around fifty observed, looking at the two of them with pleasure.

"Aunt Jemima," Mr MacPherson said, "I did not know you would be here tonight. This is Miss Campbell and, Miss Campbell, may I present my aunt, Lady Morrelly."

Ishbel curtsied. "I am happy to meet you, my lady."

"And I have been looking forward to making your acquaintance, Miss Campbell. My nephew speaks eloquently of you and the crimes you solve together when he deigns to visit me."

Mr MacPherson smiled and said, "I apologise for being haphazard in my calls upon you recently, Aunt. I will do better in future."

"Very well." She looked fondly at him and then regarded Ishbel with a kind but speculative gaze. She reached out and took Ishbel's arm. "You must tell me all about yourself, my dear. You are related to Lady Huntly, I believe."

For the next half hour, Ishbel did her best to answer several dozen questions about her family, her childhoods and her interests. Lady Morrelly showed no surprise at the fact that Ishbel attended lectures at the university, so she assumed Mr MacPherson had already mentioned this. His aunt's attitude remained friendly and welcoming during the conversation, so Ishbel had hopes that she had made a reasonable impression upon her.

Lady Morrelly then announced that the hour was a late one for her and that she would return home to her cat. As Mr MacPherson took her arm to escort her to her carriage, Lady Morrelly said to Ishbel, "I hope you will call upon me at my house, my dear."

"I would be honoured, my lady." Ishbel watched them walk away, relieved that the meeting seemed a successful one.

Mr Chiverton appeared at her side. "So you have been introduced to MacPherson's closest family. Was that arranged for tonight?"

"No, we just happened to encounter Lady Morrelly here."

"I doubt that," Chiverton said with an amused smile. "Lady Morrelly takes a strong interest in MacPherson's marital status."

Then she had come to the ball tonight just to meet Ishbel, which was an unnerving thought. "She showed no dislike of me, despite knowing of my crime work and visits to the university. She asked me to call on her, which is a good sign, surely?"

"I am quite certain she formed a good impression of you, but I should warn you that, when you next meet her, she is likely to ask why you and MacPherson are not yet engaged."

With a rush of nerves and excitement, Ishbel thought that they might possibly be engaged by the time she saw Lady Morrelly again. "How are the preparations going for your sister's coming-out ball?"

Mr Chiverton accepted the change of subject, saying, "Very well. She will be happy when she can see more of Edinburgh society and she is sensible, so I believe she will make a good choice of husband when she is ready."

There was a pause, then Ishbel said, "May I ask a favour of you?"

"Anything," he said readily.

"Could you find out about the backgrounds of all the actors in the troupe Miss McNeil belongs to?"

"Of course. Is there anything in particular you want to know?"

"I fear I am just searching for some new information or another suspect."

"MacPherson said that the investigation was only leading back to Miss McNeil. As difficult as it would be for Joe and Alex to accept, she might have actually committed the murder."

"We have asked her twice about that and I believe her when she says she is innocent."

"You are supposed to," he pointed out. "She is an actress and a good one. You would not know if she told you a lie."

Ishbel thought about Miss McNeil's confession about her argument with the duke. She had said that it was resolved, but what if it was not? What if she had only told them a partial truth and, in a moment of anger, had stabbed him with her own letter opener? It fit all the facts. She was there in the house that night. She had a motive to commit the crime. She even had a possible weapon lying on a table and had fled from the law. "You might be right."

He excused himself to invite a friend of his sister's to dance and, feeling overly warm, Ishbel walked to the end table to ask the footman stationed there for a glass of lemonade or ratafia. She reached the refreshments tables just as another lady turned away from it and found herself in the unpleasant situation of facing Lady Sarah Halsted.

"Are you still conducting your unwanted investigation into my father's murder?" the lady asked at once, although she kept her voice quiet, presumably thinking of the scandalous information they knew about her own life.

"We are, although you may soon get your wish of seeing Miss McNeil hang for the crime. It may be a hollow victory, though, since she is probably innocent, so it will mean that your father's real killer will remain free."

"You really suspected me of such a crime?" Lady Sarah sounded bewildered at the idea and Ishbel felt an unexpected moment of sympathy for her. Whatever arguments she had had with the duke, he had still been her father and this situation must be an exceedingly difficult one for her.

"We thought you might have hired someone to kill him. I am sorry."

Lady Sarah scrutinised her before saying, "If my father had any more secrets, his valet would know them. If you want to speak to him, I will tell him to answer your questions frankly."

Ishbel tried to conceal her shock at this unexpected reaction. "Thank you. We would be glad to speak to him." She saw that Mr MacPherson had returned to the ballroom and rejoined him, describing the conversation he had missed. "It seems as if Lady Sarah is willing to overlook our past suspicions about her in order to find out for certain who killed her father. This might be what we need to finally discover the truth."

The sounds of shrill voices raised in anger reached them and Ishbel looked round, but could not see or hear what was going on. A few minutes later Harriette appeared from the direction of the disturbance and answered her inquiry about it: "Sir Abbott made a remark to the effect that, if a civil war did break out in France, then the French aristocrats only had themselves to blame for it for treating the working classes so badly. You would have applauded him."

Ishbel did not deny it. "Did someone object to his comment?"

"A French lady objected most strenuously to it. There, you see: someone other than you can cause a public scene."

Harriette walked away as Ishbel began to laugh.

39. SEEKING NEW FACTS

EDDIE WAS more than happy for an excuse to spend the night with Alex instead of returning to his family's home and Miss Campbell's request gave him just that.

He had a key to the house where Alex rented a room, which was good since the large building was in darkness when he arrived. He let himself in and crept up the stairs, feeling his way in the blackness and wincing when his step on a particular board caused a loud creak. When he safely reached Alex's room without discovery, he breathed more easily.

He stood in the doorway, peering inside, and a sleepy voice said, "Who's that?"

"Me." Eddie took a step towards the voice and promptly walked into a storage trunk, stubbing his foot. "Oww!"

"Here," Alex said, sounding more awake, "I'll light a candle."

Eddie listened to the noise of rustling and then the repeated strike of flint against steel before a tiny glint of light appeared, which was transferred from tinder to candle wick. The light flared and Alex was illuminated, propped up in bed in his linen bed shirt. Alex grinned at him and held out his arms: "There – you may now make your grand entrance."

Eddie smiled and hurried to do so, closing the door behind him and crossing the room to the bed. He sat down to embrace and kiss Alex.

"This is a pleasant surprise," Alex said as Eddie stripped off his jacket and, with difficulty, removed his boots.

"Ah, I nearly forgot: I have an errand." Eddie paused in his disrobing. "Miss Campbell asked me to find out from you information about the past of all the actors in your troupe."

Alex frowned. "She thinks an actor killed the duke?"

146

"I do not think she knows who to suspect. Kenina's trial is fast approaching and they have disproved others of the crime." He turned and touched his beloved's arm, running his hand up and down it and feeling the curve of light muscle. "You might have to brace yourself for a difficult end to this matter. It does not sound as if there is much hope left for Kenina."

"No, the jury can't convict an innocent person." Alex's brow furrowed and he looked sick at the idea.

"Are you utterly sure she did not kill him?"

The frown was turned upon him. "Your instinctive reaction when you first heard of the murder was to say she could not have done it. Why would you think differently now?"

"MacPherson and Miss Campbell have proven that there was no burglar who could have killed him, the servants had no reason to harm him and, in my mind, that really only leaves Kenina." He stood up to remove his breeches.

"The duke must have invited someone in himself."

"In the middle of the night? Who?"

Alex rubbed a finger over his lower lip as he sat considering this. "He had any number of acquaintances and he was not the kind of person to turn away someone in need of help. I suppose it could have been one of the more recently hired actors, although it gives me goosebumps to think that I might have been working alongside a murderer. An actor might show up at Kenina's house in the middle of the night if they had a good enough reason."

Eddie got into the bed just as Alex left it. "Where are you going?" he complained.

Alex patted his chest. "I want to write down a response to Miss Campbell's request." He gave Eddie a teasing look as he got up. "You will have to exercise patience."

Eddie smiled and folded his arms behind his head to wait.

40. HOPE LOST

ISHBEL WAS re-reading the letters sent to Miss McNeil by her acting friend while Harriette made derisive comments about the contents of one of Edinburgh's broadsheets, when Mr Chiverton was announced.

He joined them in the drawing room and bowed gracefully before offering a charming smile. It occurred to Ishbel that it must be difficult for the perfectly respectable-looking Mr McDonald to have two such handsome friends. Mr Chiverton was even more striking in his plainer daywear than his grand ball clothes and with his own blond hair instead of a wig. The personalities of the men were very different too, although Mr MacPherson and Mr Chiverton both seemed more outgoing than their friend, and she wondered how they had met.

"Miss Campbell, regarding your request at the ball," he said, accepting a drink of chocolate and taking a seat with the ladies, "this is a letter from Mr Aldridge that should answer all your questions about the actors."

She accepted the letter he held out, wondering who Mr Aldridge was and how she was supposed to know of him.

"He included as much information as he knows and hopes it will assist you, although he naturally hopes none of the troupe are involved in the duke's death."

Realisation struck her at the casual way he spoke of the man: Mr Aldridge was his close friend, whom she had heard mentioned as Alex. She wondered when he had seen him between the ball and this morning in order to get the letter, then had an idea of the answer and decided, feeling a blush rise to her cheeks, that she had better not consider the matter further.

"I am grateful to you for bringing it to me so quickly," she said.

"I am happy to help."

Harriette asked him about his family and, while he was replying, Ishbel broke the seal on the letter and opened it, skimming the two-sided list of facts about the actors. It was just what she had wanted, giving the information she needed to send a further letter of inquiry to the relevant office in England.

"That is kind of you, Lady Huntly," Mr Chiverton was saying and these struck Ishbel as unlikely words for anyone to utter to Harriette, so she wondered what she had missed.

He stood up to take his leave of them and Ishbel said, "Would you thank Mr Aldridge for his letter. The information is most useful."

"Good. I will pass that on."

He left and Ishbel asked Harriette, "What was Mr Chiverton thanking you for a minute ago?"

"Had you been listening to your own guest, as politeness would expect you to, then you would know the answer to that," Harriette told her and went downstairs to order the servants about.

Ishbel walked into the library and sat down at the mahogany writing desk. She carefully read through Mr Aldridge's letter again, then got out several sheets of paper, quill, ink and pot of sand and wrote three short letters. She had just sprinkled sand on the last letter, to dry the ink, when Mr MacPherson was announced. She shook the sand off, folded the letters, poured wax onto them and sealed them with the family crest.

Mr MacPherson came in as she handed the letters to the butler for sending out and she said, "Mr Chiverton was here just before you."

She gave him Mr Aldridge's letter and he looked it over. "Is there an actor you suspect of the murder?"

"Not really, but I wondered if there might be something relevant in the relationships between the actors. It was just an idea and might be nothing, but we should have further information to consider in a few days."

"In the meantime, shall we call upon Lady Sarah before she changes her mind about allowing us to interview the Duke of Raden's valet?"

"Gladly. While it is unlikely that he knows the actual name of the murderer, I am hopeful that our talk with him will help us solve the crime."

They took Mr MacPherson's carriage to Lady Sarah Halsted's house and were admitted to a small room. As they waited for the valet

Ishbel wandered over to the window. The sun had melted most of the frost and it was a bright, pleasant day. She saw two figures on the path of the formal garden and recognised them as Lady Sarah and Lord Moray.

"Perhaps they will marry now," she commented and Mr MacPherson joined her at the window.

"I hope so," he answered, "but I doubt the duke would have objected to the courtship if he had thought marriage would be the result."

"Then Lord Moray has probably been deceiving Lady Sarah with the same kinds of lies the duke told Miss McNeil: that he wants to always be with her and can imagine no life without her. What would have happened to Miss McNeil if the duke had ended the relationship? Her life would have changed drastically. Where would she live? How would she survive?"

"You forget that she received a wage for her acting work," Mr MacPherson reminded her. "She must have lived on that before meeting the duke and his previous mistress did say that he left her with a generous sum of money."

"But how would that compare to the idea he waved in front of her that she could be a duchess?"

"Badly."

An unexpected thought made her smile at him. "Can you believe that not many months ago, neither of us had any connection with murders, corpses, duels or physical altercations?"

"I do recall that my life was rather a dull one before I met you."

"And mine was a lonely one," she confessed, smile fading, "haunted by memories from my childhood of my parents' unhappy marriage. I dwelt too much on it. When you proposed to me..."

The door opened and, with the worst timing imaginable, a man came into the room and apologised for keeping them waiting. The valet – former valet, as he told them he was now working as a footman here until he could find a new position – was a smart, thin faced man with a lilting Highlands accent.

"I worked as his grace's valet for more than ten years," he told them, "and the master trusted me to be discreet, so I knew more than most about his life."

"You knew that Miss McNeil had become his mistress?" Mr MacPherson asked.

The valet glanced uncomfortably at Ishbel, before replying, "Aye. I assisted the duke in finding a house for the, er, lady involved and I would deliver and receive the letters that passed between them."

"Did the duke say anything to you that might help us find his killer?" Ishbel asked.

"I have thought about the matter, miss, and find it difficult to believe that Miss McNeil coulda done such a thing. She was always civil to me and her servants spoke well of her, saying she was kind and considerate. Some women in, er, that situation were more interested in the money than the duke, but she seemed to genuinely love him and he treated her well."

"Did you know that they argued before he died?" she asked.

"Aye." He would not meet her eyes, clearly awkward at discussing such matters as a pregnancy out of wedlock with an unmarried lady.

"Do you know if the disagreement was resolved?"

"Och, aye. The duke went out and spent a small fortune on a necklace for her the day before he died as an apology for what he'd said. After he came back from her house he was in a sunny mood all right."

"When did he leave on the night he died?" Mr MacPherson asked.

"Later than he intended. Not much before midnight."

"Was he alone?" Ishbel queried.

"Aye, Miss Campbell."

"Then had he arranged to meet anyone else?"

"No, miss."

"But, if Miss McNeil did not kill him, he must have let his murderer into the house. Did he not mention anyone else?"

"No." He frowned. "He wanted to see Kenina. It isna likely anyone else woulda accompanied him there and I can think of no one else who would visit the lady's house after midnight."

Then their trip here had been pointless. She fought back a wave of disappointment, her mind picturing Miss McNeil sitting in her gaol room, relying on them to save her. She swallowed.

"Thank you for your help," Mr MacPherson was saying to the valet.

"I liked the duke, sir. I wish I knew more about what happened to him."

They left the house, only to find one of Mr MacPherson's footmen hurrying up the steps to meet them.

"The jury are ready to give their verdict about Viscount Inderly," he said with breathless excitement.

She and Mr MacPherson exchanged glances before he thanked the footman and sent him home, then ordered his carriage driver to take them to the court as swiftly as possible. Ishbel sat beside him, sick at the thought of going back into the courtroom where her family's good name had been further attacked, but eager to know the outcome of the case.

The carriage came to a halt too quickly and Ishbel froze, suddenly unable to bear the thought that the viscount might be found innocent. Mr MacPherson held out his hand to help her down from the carriage and, looking into his face, she somehow found the courage to take it and walk inside with him. Harriette was waiting for them and Ishbel had never been so happy to see her. She also caught sight of Mr and Mrs Jones, taking seats halfway down the courtroom, behind a group of indifferent, chattering people who were probably just here to enjoy the scandal.

She sat down with Mr MacPherson and Harriette, only to have to stand up again as the judge arrived. Ishbel dug her fingernails into her palm as she waited. This had been their first case and she wanted so badly to get some form of justice to help Mr and Mrs Jones cope with the loss of their daughter.

The judge asked the jury whether they had found the defendant guilty or not guilty and the room went silent, a tension in it that was almost palpable.

Ishbel closed her eyes as she waited for the answer, breathing in short, shallow spurts.

The foreman spoke quietly, making them strain to hear him. "We find the defendant guilty."

Ishbel nearly laughed aloud, such was her relief. All their work had had a positive outcome after all. Around them, people were talking about the verdict, but she could do no more than exchange smiles with Mr MacPherson and Harriette, feeling weak now that the case was over.

The judge pounded his gavel on the wooden surface in front of him and silence fell once more. He turned his gaze upon Viscount Inderly. "You have been found guilty of the crimes of reckless endangerment and hiring an unlicensed doctor, but given the mitigating factors of your youth, background and previous good character, I sentence you to pay a fine of one hundred pounds."

Ishbel stared at him in disbelief. A fine? That was all?

"The important thing is that he was found guilty," Harriette told her, taking her hand. "You should be happy about that."

Happiness was not even a distant relation of the emotion she was feeling. Her gaze sought out Mr and Mrs Jones and Ishbel saw that Aileas's mother was crying. Ishbel had trusted that justice would be done and had given Mr and Mrs Jones false hope of the same, and that faith had been destroyed.

41. SEARCHING FOR THE MISSING PIECE

EWAN CALLED upon Miss Campbell the next day to discuss the duke's death and they ate an early luncheon together. He observed her carefully as they spoke, still concerned over the pain-filled look that had been in her eyes yesterday when the verdict was given in the Aileas Jones trial.

Miss Campbell stared with an unseeing gaze at her plate of scones. "I keep thinking that we already have the solution to the murder, but we are unable to see it. So far we have had three possible people who seemed worth considering for the duke's death: Lord Moray, Lady Sarah and Mrs Ainsley."

"Mrs Ainsley never had a strong motive, would never have committed the murder herself and did not hire anyone else, except in connection with a robbery, so she is certainly innocent," Ewan said, wishing he could find a way to get the conversation back to what Miss Campbell had been about to say yesterday morning about his proposal. It sounded as if she might have been saying she regretted turning him down, but perhaps that was just what he wanted to believe. However, even if she had simply wanted to tell him her reasons for refusing him, he would like to hear them and understand what he had done wrong. "Lord Moray and Lady Sarah provided alibis for each other for the entire night when the duke was killed."

"Only if they committed the murder themselves."

"If it was Lord Moray then why would he take such a dangerous chance as to involve anyone else? He could have easily killed the duke himself, but he never left his house. Similarly, if Lady Sarah wanted her father dead then why would she not turn to Lord Moray, who was already angry with the duke? Who else could she have asked to do the murder for her? None of the servants spoke very well of her to Rabbie, and they liked the duke far better, so I cannot believe it was one of them."

"Perhaps she tricked one of her would-be suitors into killing for her," Miss Campbell said and took a bite of scone. "She could have said she would marry him if he did this. If she never actually intended to marry her paramour, Lord Moray, then she could still do it."

"There were several men interested in marrying her," Ewan recalled, holding the porcelain cup of tea in his hands to warm them, "but she is helping us."

"Or sending us looking in a different direction," Miss Campbell said, then pulled a face, "but it is unlikely she would have her father's valet speak freely to us if she still had secrets to hide. She has the best motive out of everyone connected with the duke, though. What if she did, in fact, know about her father's dalliance with Miss McNeil? The staff thought she was unaware of it, but Lord Moray knew. He could have told her."

"Then why did he not commit the murder?" Ewan asked.

"The duke was a former friend of his. Perhaps he did not have the heart to do it."

"But he had the heart to spend the night with Lady Sarah, both of them knowing the duke was being killed while they were together? She would have known she might be suspected of the crime so it would have been more sensible for her to remain at her own home and make sure the servants saw her there."

She put down her teacup with a slight clatter. "You are right. Unless the maid tells us something new or is guilty of the crime herself, we have no suspects left except for Miss McNeil."

"What about your inquiry concerning the actors?"

"I have not yet heard back from the offices in England. I have no definite suspicion, but it might still help us."

She sounded unconvinced about this and Ewan watched her as he thought about what they did and did not know.

"What if someone saw the murderer?" Miss Campbell said.

"We spoke to the staff at Miss McNeil's house..." he began.

"No, I do not mean them. What if someone saw the duke's arrival? What if they saw the person whom he let into the house?"

"It was late at night, but it is possible."

"Some people work late hours. Others sleep on the streets."

Ewan got up. "I will send for Jed and see if he can help us."

They spoke to the young caddie an hour later and he left with a promise to learn anything he could. Ewan hoped they would finally discover something useful, all too aware of the sand running out in the hourglass of Kenina McNeil's life.

42. AN UNWELCOME DISCOVERY

ISHBEL WAS due to attend a lecture at the university at midday the next morning, so Mr MacPherson called to see her with Jed Cassell just after breakfast.

"I tried to find out if anyone had seen the duke arrive home or anyone who might have been with him, but I had no luck there. It's a quieter, more respectable street, so there are few people about late at night. If it helps any, it's likely he arrived there on foot as a carriage woulda be heard."

They had already known that his coachman had not driven him anywhere. Miss McNeil's house would only have been a fifteen or twenty minute walk from his own.

"Could he have hired someone to light the way for him?" Mr MacPherson asked.

"I asked about that, sir, and none of the regular laddies took him there."

"Is it at all possible that a thief could have got a key to the house?" Ishbel asked, thinking of what Marie had said. "Could someone who worked on the locks have got a key and let themselves into Miss McNeil's house, only to be surprised by the duke and kill him?"

"I could ask if any locksmith worked at the house, miss."

They had nothing better to look into that she could think of, so she said yes to this and the men left. She was reading through the notes she had made since the start of the case when Harriette walked into the library.

"You will render yourself blind from the amount of time you spend reading," her cousin commented.

She ignored this and said, "Miss McNeil's trial will shortly start and we have nothing. If the case goes unsolved and she hangs for it..."

"That would not be your fault," Harriette said, walking across the room to sit opposite her.

"Then whose? We should have done better than this. We were supposed to find justice for those who might otherwise be denied it, but we have failed."

"Perhaps there was nothing to find and the facts were exactly as they appeared from the start. If Miss McNeil is hanged, it probably means that she is guilty."

She was saved from giving an answer to this by the arrival of the butler, who brought in two letters for her on a silver tray. She took them and thanked him as Harriette left, then broke the seals and read them. The second letter she read again, its contents not what she had expected. She had had a vague thought that Miss McNeil might have had a husband amongst the actors, someone she had parted from but who still had a reason to kill over her.

She frowned down at the parchment as she realised that she had indeed found a motive for the duke's death, although she sought for a reason to discount it.

She raised her eyes, gazing sightlessly at the shelves of books in front of her. Some instinct had put the fear in her mind that this case would end badly and she wished now that they had never taken it. This outcome was the worst one she could imagine and, as she thought of everyone who would be hurt by the truth, her mood sank even lower.

She had not moved when Mr MacPherson arrived. "Ishbel!" he exclaimed, striding across the room to kneel in front of her chair. "Miss Campbell, are you ill? You look white. Should I send for a physician?"

She looked into his kind eyes and knew this would make him unhappy too. She had the wild thought that she could lie and tear up the letter, but the result of that was unthinkable. "I know who the killer is and I very much wish that I did not."

"What do you mean?" He got up and pulled a chair close to hers, leaning towards her.

"We have been going round in circles, when the answer was there almost from the start. Ewan, what is the one thing that a good actor knows how to do?"

43. WHAT HAPPENED THAT NIGHT

JOE FILLINISTER and Miss McNeil were waiting for them inside the room of the dark, filthy gaol, when Ishbel and Ewan arrived.

"Have you discovered something?" Miss McNeil asked, pale and worried.

"Yes," Ishbel told her. "We know who killed the Duke of Raden."

"Then you know it was me," she said at once. "I knew your investigation could do me no good, but Joe was so desperate to help me. I was furious at the duke..."

"Kenina, stop," Mr Fillinister said, putting a hand on her arm. "This is pointless."

"You realised the truth when we were last here," Ishbel said, heart going out to the distressed woman. "You covered it up by pretending to faint, but we had asked you who knew about the duke's callous treatment of you. That was when you put the pieces together."

"I killed him."

"No, you did not," Ishbel said, feeling sick because she knew that Miss McNeil would rather hang than see the real culprit die. They had wanted to help her and it was impossible. "While you were miserable over the duke's behaviour and terrified of bringing an illegitimate child into the world, you turned to the one person you always turned to: Mr Fillinister, your brother."

"How did you find out?" he asked in a calm voice and, looking at him, she saw for the first time the resemblance between the siblings; the same dark hair and blue eyes. They even had the same accent but, knowing they were both born in England, she had never thought it unusual.

"I thought we might be missing something about Miss McNeil's relationships with the other actors. I half-thought she might have been married to one of the men but, of course, actors often change their names. Fillinister was your father's surname and McNeil was your mother's maiden name. We believed at the start that someone could have killed the duke out of love for Miss McNeil and that was what happened."

"Yes," he agreed, stepping closer to his sister and taking her hand. "I was always worried about Kenina's relationship with the duke, that such a powerful man would leave her one day, but he seemed so honest in his affection for her that I was fooled. When Kenina came and told me she thought she was going to have a child and that that bastard had yelled at her and was going to leave her... I've never hated anyone so much in my life."

"What happened that night?"

"I went to the house to check on Kenina. She'd been inconsolable and I was afraid of what she might do. But I was delayed at the theatre and when I got to her house all the rooms were dark, so I realised she must be asleep. I was leaving when I saw the duke." Mr Fillinister shook his head, features screwed up with pain. "I couldn't believe he'd just go back there as if nothing had happened, after the way he'd treated her. It was obvious that it could only end with him leaving her, now or later, heartbroken."

"What did you say to him?" Mr MacPherson asked.

"Nothing. I didn't have to. He greeted me with pleasure as if nothing had changed and invited me inside. I think he wanted a drinking companion. I had the knife in my pocket for protection – almost all the troupe carry one – so I just stabbed him. He took a while to die and I nearly changed my mind and called for a doctor, seeing him in agony like that, then suddenly it was over. I didn't think how it would look, him being in her house like that. I just panicked and ran out."

"But the next day Miss McNeil came to your house," Ishbel prompted, shaking him out of whatever dark memories he was lost in.

"Yes. I'd paced back and forth all night, trying to decide what we should do. Kenina wanted to run and I realised that was the only thing that'd keep her out of gaol. I gave her money to leave, intending to follow when I knew if she was going to get the blame. I almost turned myself in, but I thought that if we could only get abroad, we might survive."

"Why did you come to us?" Mr MacPherson asked.

"I just wanted you to prove she couldn't have killed him. Even if you thought someone else was guilty, there would be no evidence, so they wouldn't hang. I never would've let the trial begin – I would've confessed before then. You know that, don't you?" he said to Kenina.

She embraced him, tears running down her cheeks. "Of course I do. You just wanted to protect me, as you always do. It wasn't your fault." She turned to Ishbel and Mr MacPherson. "Please don't tell the law it was him, I beg you."

"They have to," Mr Fillinister said, kissing her forehead. "I can't let you die for my crime. I'd hoped to get away with it, that no one would be found guilty, but the law will do what it wants with me now."

He had an arm round her waist and she was leaning her head against his shoulder.

That was how she and Mr MacPherson left them, sharing a moment of affection, before they had him arrested for murder.

44. A BAD DECISION

"DID YOU have any success?" Ishbel asked as soon as Mr MacPherson arrived the next morning.

He took the seat beside hers in the dining room. "Because of Joe Fillinister's confession, Miss McNeil has been released."

That had been a certainty and was not what had kept her awake worrying for much of the night. "Yes, but did the solicitors listen to you about Mr Fillinister only acting as he did out of love for his sister? Will it stop him being hanged?"

The bleak look on his face answered her question. "The solicitor defending Joe will certainly allow Miss McNeil and me to speak for him at the trial. It might make a difference."

It would not. She had held out little hope before, but now it was gone. It felt as if they were placing the noose around his neck themselves. "We are responsible for this."

"We had no choice," he said, touching her arm for a moment and almost distracting her from her fears. "We took on this investigation to bring the Duke of Raden's killer to justice."

She pulled away, angry at herself and him for believing in such a simplistic idea. "This is not justice, nor anything close to it."

"Miss McNeil is out of gaol and safe now."

"Her life is ruined. If she has to watch her brother die after everything else she has gone through, she will never recover."

"Whatever his reasons, Joe killed someone. He must pay for it."

She twisted a handkerchief between her hands. "If he had killed someone working class with good reason, then he might well face transportation or lose a hand. Because he murdered a duke he will certainly hang. How is that fair?"

"We had no choice," he repeated.

"Yes, we did," she insisted. "We should never have got involved in this kind of work. I thought we could help people, but we have done the opposite."

"Only on this occasion," he argued. "We found out what happened to Aileas, which helped her family."

"And her killer was released with only a fine."

"He did not deliberately murder her."

"And he was a viscount," she said bitterly. She jumped up from her chair, unable to remain still any longer, and walked over to the window.

"What can I do?" Mr MacPherson asked quietly.

She looked back into his concerned eyes and felt only confusion. She had been ready to marry him and she had been sure that what they were doing was right. "I need to take some time to decide whether I want to continue solving crimes. If we do more harm than good, then it is meaningless."

"You should do whatever is best for you," he said and part of her wanted to throw herself into his arms. She knew that nothing was more important to him than her happiness; his actions had made that clear time and again. Her actions, on the other hand, had wrecked her own reputation and, were she ever to marry him, would damage his standing in society. It had not seemed so important when she thought they were doing something useful and necessary, but now she could not help thinking how much easier his life would be if he married someone else.

But she loved him.

She swallowed, the words like ashes in her mouth as she said, "I think that we should not see each other at all for the time being."

The expression in his eyes made her heart ache. "Surely I could still call here as your friend?"

"Our entire relationship is based around our working partnership. Without that, we would have to rediscover who we are and what we have in common."

"I thought we had more together than the work." He looked pale, strong cheekbones standing out sharply in his face. "After everything we have said to each other and endured together..." He tailed off and got abruptly to his feet.

"Ewan, I am so sorry."

He bowed to her as though to a stranger. "Good day, Miss Campbell."

She watched him turn and walk towards the door and everything in her said to go after him and take back her words, but she did not know any more if she belonged in his life.

He left the room and, seconds later, she heard the front door click shut behind him.

What had she done?

Thanks for reading

Thank you so much for taking an interest in my books. If you enjoyed this novel please would you consider leaving a review at Amazon or Goodreads, as this is a massive help to independent authors in getting our books known. It also helps other readers learn more about the books, so they can decide whether to buy them.

Join the Fun

If you join my email group at my website, clarejayne.com, you will get various gifts as a thank you. These include a free novella, **"Harriette"**, which tells of the events which turn a naive young woman into the fierce Lady Huntly from the *Campbell & MacPherson* novels. You will also get a sequel to my historical romance, **"Complications"** and a guide to the historical world and characters from the *Campbell & MacPherson* series. I will also let you know about my upcoming novels and I'll share special offers and freebies from myself and other authors.

OTHER NOVELS AVAILABLE AT AMAZON

"Lady Tinbough's Dilemma (Campbell & MacPherson 1)" - Ishbel is interested in only her studies. Ewan is interested in only Ishbel. They make the unlikeliest detectives imaginable.

Ishbel Campbell lives in Georgian era Edinburgh and hates the uselessness of high society life with its constant balls and dinner parties, escaping it by the shocking means of attending lectures at the city's university. She decided long ago that she would never marry. With the wealth of a large estate to give him a life of luxury, Ewan MacPherson loves this world and believes the only thing missing from it is a wife.

Ishbel and Ewan meet at the trial of masked gentleman thief, William Brodie. This interest in crime leads to them being given the task of finding a missing emerald necklace. Ishbel only agrees to appease her cousin and Ewan only does so to spend more time with Ishbel. With no idea of what they are doing, they are close to giving up when they discover that a young maid has disappeared. In a time before the police force ever existed, no one but them cares about the fate of a working class woman, so they are determined to find her.

As the danger rises and jealousies and insecurities threaten their partnership, will they be able to solve the mystery in time or will the criminal's deadly attentions turn on them?

"The Dead Duke (Campbell & MacPherson 2)" - When Ishbel and Ewan take on the case of a duke supposedly murdered by his actress mistress, Lady Huntly threatens to disown Ishbel while Edinburgh's upper classes are appalled, and that is before the duo even begin looking into the reasons why the wealthiest members of society might have wanted the duke dead.

As they continue to uncover secrets others want to remain hidden, their own relationship is threatened by the public discovery of a scandal from Ishbel's past. Is her repeated refusal to follow society's conventions about to ruin her life as well as her partnership with Ewan, and will they ever manage to solve the mystery of who murdered the duke?

"A Dangerous Past (Campbell & MacPherson 3)" – When

Ishbel agrees to help her lady's maid, Lucy, find out why a friend of hers was killed, Ishbel must find a way to end the estrangement between herself and Ewan so they can work together again. Their relationship quickly improves until the arrival of Ewan's sister, who is determined he should end his investigations into crimes as well as his association with Ishbel.

"The Convenient Murder (Campbell & MacPherson 4)" - The unconventional Georgian-era detectives, Ishbel and Ewan, have a new murder to investigate when Lord Strand is poisoned at a house where their friends, Miss Chiverton and McDonald, are staying.

Miss Chiverton seems determined that the murder be solved, so why is she hiding important information about it? Lord Strand's relatives all appear more relieved than grief-stricken over the death and everyone who ever met the man seems to have hated him, so the list of suspects is endless.

In the meantime, Miss Chiverton's father is determined that she should make a decision about who to marry or he will choose for her. The man who is desperately in love with her is the last person she wants and all she can focus on is helping to solve the murder.

As events grow more hazardous, lives change and not everyone will emerge unscathed.

"Mr Guthrie's Double (Campbell & MacPherson 5)" - A killer is about to strike but which Mr Guthrie is he after?

Ishbel and Ewan, are given a bizarre new case when they have to hunt down an imposter who has been falsely claiming to be Mr Guthrie.

The real Mr Guthrie is a likeable man from a wealthy family who wins the affection of Miss Chiverton. This complicates everyone's lives as Ewan's friend, Mr McDonald, also loves her and her family only approves of Mr McDonald as a suitor, so Miss Chiverton will face a difficult decision about her future.

The case soon grows more strange and more deadly when a corpse is found, but it won't be the last death as Ishbel and Ewan desperately work to uncover the reason for the impersonator's deception.

"A Virtuous Man (Campbell & MacPherson 6)" - Why would a seemingly honourable university student vanish one night and never return home?

After Ishbel and Ewan leave Edinburgh, the newly married Mr and Mrs McDonald inherit their missing person case, much to Padraig's annoyance. He is sure the young man must have gone off alone to have fun and Padraig would rather concentrate on life with his new bride than deal with it. The missing man is a devout Catholic, though, so it seems increasingly unlikely that he ran off in this way. They then discover that a second man went missing on the same night as the first.

As the missing person case grows more baffling, it causes arguments between Fiona and Padraig - whose marriage might not be as stable as they thought - and the longer the matter remains unsolved, the more likely it is that the boy will die before they can find him.

"An Impossible Crime (Campbell & MacPherson 7)" - Things are not going well for Ishbel and Ewan. Ishbel is miserable living in the countryside, Ewan hates how much time she spends with the local physician and they have a new murder to solve.

Ishbel was looking forward to returning to Edinburgh soon, but now that plan has had to be changed. She is bored and frustrated living on the country estate where Ewan grew up, while he has plenty to do and spends little time at home. She only has two real friends nearby – James Fraser, a physician, and Emma Lee, a spinster.

It is James who tells them of Lady Ashton's death and of his professional belief that she was smothered with a pillow. Both Lady Ashton's husband and cousin had reasons to kill her, but unfortunately it seems impossible for them to have done so.

James takes an interest in their hunt for the killer, Ewan growing less civil every time he finds him at the house, and then Emma falls under suspicion for the crime. Tensions rise between Ishbel and Ewan to the point where their marriage is threatened and a final twist might have even more devastating consequences for them.

"The Prankster (Campbell & MacPherson 8)" - When is a joke not a joke?

Miss Emma Lee, neighbour to Ishbel and Ewan, is being disturbed by a series of bizarre pranks involving her late father's hat.

Unnerved by it and bemused as to why she is the unknown culprit's target, she turns to the duo for help.

They are still living on their country estate, Ishbel having given birth to Meg, their second child, recently. Emma is one of Ishbel's closest friends and she and Ewan believe this will be a quick, safe mystery to solve, bringing no danger to their family. They are wrong on both accounts.

When the prankster's tricks turn deadly, no one is safe. The amateur detectives must use all their skills to protect their neighbours and their own lives whilst solving the riddle of who is responsible and why.

"Murder on Bealtaine Eve (Dumnonia Mysteries 1)" With blood spilt during a sacred ceremony, will the gods forgive her people?

In fifth century Dark Ages England, Morvoren is the priestess of Dumnonia, serving the goddess who protects them. She is confident of her place as one of the most important people in the tribe, with the respect of the king and love of her people. At least, that's what she thinks.

The inexplicable murder of a Saxon guest throws all her assumptions about her life into confusion and makes her fear retribution from her goddess. Forced to work with Uxio, a young Christian deacon who hates her religion, she must solve the crime or lose her home and her freedom.

Uxio is ordered to work with Morvoren by his bishop, but this tribe brings back far too many memories of a past he has tried to forget. Morvoren's uncanny ability to see more than he wants to reveal puts them at odds and a second murder adds to the tension between them. With the possibility of war between the Dumnonii and the Saxons looming over them, they struggle to hunt down an elusive killer.

This unique historical mystery series is set against the backdrop of Celtic beliefs and one tribe's struggle to survive in the changing land of Britannia.

"Fatal Voyage (Dumnonia Mysteries 2)" - Will Morvoren and Uxio discover a killer or a vengeful ghost?

With the approach of the Samhain festival to honour the dead, the captain of a merchant ship tells Morvoren an eerie tale of a voyage plagued by misfortune, illness and death, wanting her, as Dumnonia's priestess, to help rid him of its source. The captain is sure that the two deaths are from natural causes, since no one could have got to the second man, whose body was found blocking the door to his cabin. Despite this, the Christian deacon, Uxio believes the problems are the result of a murderer onboard.

Circumstances and their different personalities cause Uxio and Morvoren to quarrel yet again over how to find out the truth, so they make a wager to investigate the mystery separately. Each one will try to be the first to discover how two people on the ship died.

There seems to be no link between the dead men and no way for them to have been murdered, but both had their enemies. As Morvoren and Uxio struggle to make sense of the mystery, what fresh troubles will they face? They are both determined to best the other, but will a killer outwit them both?

This is the second novel in this exciting historical mystery series set in the Celtic Dumnonii tribe in England in the Dark Ages, a time of turmoil with conflicting beliefs and cultures.

"The Vanishing Thief (Dumnonia Mysteries 3)" - How could someone disappear from a castle on a cliff with stolen treasure, never being seen by the guards at its only entrance?

The latest mystery infuriates the king, confuses the warriors protecting the castle and needs to be solved by Morvoren and Uxio. While Morvoren deals with a problem with her closest friend and Uxio struggles to cope with a servant with a crush on him, they must somehow work out how the impossible theft was committed.

The subsequent appearance of a dead body doesn't help in the least.

"Murder By Another Name (Dumnonia Mysteries 4)" - When is a crime not a crime? Morvoren, the priestess of the Dumnonii in Dark Age Britain, has to travel most of the length to solve a new mystery that the chieftan, Comux, can't deal with. Kenosaglas has killed his life-long friend, Eudaf, claiming that Eudaf was a spy for the nearby Saxons. If Kenosaglas is telling the truth then he cannot be punished for his actions. If he killed Eudaf for another reason, Kenosaglas is a murderer who will probably face execution.

Morvoren faces a seemingly unsolvable puzzle since no one witnessed Eudaf's death except for his killer. Even the two men's families can tell her nothing helpful and Kenosaglas's own children insist that Eudaf was not a traitor. Her search for the truth leads her to another confrontation with the Saxon leader who once wanted to marry her.

In the meantime, the Christian deacon Uxio has been left behind at Bran Castle and has a reunion that leaves his future in question.

The danger increases for Morvoren, who is under the protection of Comux, the son of the queen who hates her. When her life depends on it, will she be able to trust him?

"**Ladies Dancing**" - Three people find romance over a magical winter season.

In Regency England Kate and Louisa arrive in London - accompanied by Kate's brother, Will - to make their debuts into London society and find themselves husbands. Kate encounters Mr Templeton, who is the opposite of everything she thinks she wants in a man. He might soon change her mind, though, if her blunt manners do not ruin everything.

Her cousin, Louisa, wants to get a wealthy husband as quickly as possible for her own secret reasons. Why she should soon decide to turn down a good-natured earl is a mystery and Kate is determined to find out what she is hiding. The truth might prove to be more than she can cope with.

There is also her brother, Will, to worry about. As a wealthy, attractive gentleman, he could easily find himself a wife... if only he did not loathe every person he encounters, with the notable exception of the charming Mr Fenton. To make the best of the situation, Kate intends to throw the two men at each other as much as possible to keep Will from scaring off their potential suitors. She never imagines the attachment that might form between Will and Mr Fenton.

Just as the duo are making progress in their romantic adventures, a scandal is revealed that threatens to devastate their lives.

If you enjoy the romance, family drama and humour of a Georgette Heyer story, you will love this festive historical novel.

"**Complications**" - This is a light-hearted Georgian era romance where, in the hunt for the right gentleman, nothing works out as intended.

Amelia Daventry dreams of having the lovely clothes and luxuries her family cannot afford. She intends to use her Edinburgh season to get herself the wealthiest and most powerful husband she can find. The one thing of which she is certain is that Mr Brightford, with his constant frowns and criticisms, is a man she would never consider.

Amelia's best friend, Lottie Harrington, has found the man she wants to marry and just wishes to live quietly and make him happy. Her hopes are about to be destroyed, causing pain and chaos to herself and everyone around her.

Lottie's headstrong brother, Benjamin Harrington, has romantic feelings for other men but his parents still expect him to marry. When he meets a man he can love he faces difficult choices but does the gentleman even return his affection?

From suffering heartbreak and tragedy to fighting a duel, the lives of these three friends are about to become extremely complicated...

"An Impetuous Romance" - Will Adam bring Eloise happiness or break her heart?

Miss Eloise Preston is thrilled when the kind, handsome Lord Adam Delworth arrives in Somerset and shows an interest in her, unaware that his offer of marriage has just been turned down by someone he believes to have been the love of his life. To get her out of a dangerous situation, he asks her to marry him and, believing that he loves her, she gladly agrees.

They go to London accompanied by her sisters, Maddie and Helena. Adam immediately encounters his first love again and he is torn between the two women. In the meantime, London society - with its own rules of conduct - is causing the sisters to make one blunder after another. To add to their problems, Helena Preston is thrown into the company of the man she rejected, whom her father is determined she should still marry.

The lives and loves of Eloise, Adam, Helena and Maddie are all connected in this heart-warming Regency romance. If you enjoy the humour, twists and turns, and gentle romance of a Georgette Heyer novel, this is the perfect book for you.

ABOUT THE AUTHOR

Clare Jayne began writing novels nearly three decades ago, when she was a teenager. She has worked in a variety of jobs, including legal secretary and sales advisor, while continuing to write and trying and failing to get a traditional publisher for her work. She then had a short play performed by the local amateur dramatics group and recorded on local radio, and she came joint first place in a writing competition. This encouraged her to take a leap of faith and self-publish and she is thrilled to finally be able to share her novels with actual real people.

Inspired by such writers as Jane Austen, Josephine Tey and Georgette Heyer, she writes historical romances and historical mysteries (although the mysteries also have a strong dash of romance).

You can find out more about Clare Jayne at her website (clarejayne.com) or on Facebook, Twitter or Goodreads.

Printed in Great Britain
by Amazon

62686168R00102